THE CHALLENGE

"Since I'm here, Foreman," Clint said, "we'd better have a talk. I intend to leave this town with Jill Church, without you and your friends on our trail."

"And how do you intend to do that? We're free to travel in any direction we want."

"Except mine."

"And you're gonna stop us?" Foreman asked. "All four of us?"

"Yes," Clint said. "All four of you."

"To stop us," Foreman said, "you'd have to kill us all."

Clint smiled. . . .

THE GUNSMITH

190

LADY ON THE RUN

J. R. ROBERTS

JOVE BOOKS, NEW YORK

LADY ON THE RUN

A Jove Book / published by arrangement with
the author

PRINTING HISTORY
Jove edition / October 1997

The Putnam Berkley World Wide Web site address is
http://www.berkley.com

ISBN: 0-515-12163-0

A JOVE BOOK®
Jove Books are published by The Berkley Publishing Group,
a member of Penguin Putnam Inc.,
200 Madison Avenue, New York, New York 10016.
JOVE and the "J" design are trademarks
belonging to Jove Publications, Inc.

PRINTED IN THE UNITED STATES OF AMERICA

10 9 8 7 6 5 4 3 2 1

PROLOGUE

Jill Church crept quietly out the window, trying not to make even the slightest sound. She didn't hold out much hope for this escape attempt, but she was going to give it her best try, nevertheless.

Once outside the ground-floor window she reached in for the sack she'd left on the floor. It held some meager supplies that she hoped to make last a few days until she reached a town.

With the sack in hand she crept along the side of the building until she reached the back, then moved silently along the back until she reached the other side. She could hear the sounds coming from inside the house, the laughter, the shouting, the other women. She could even hear the sound of the poker chips striking each other as they landed in the center of the table. She had waited a long time for this poker game to come, to mask her escape. She hoped that the men in the house would be so wrapped up in their cards and their whores that they wouldn't notice she was gone until morning—maybe even later, if they drank enough.

This was going to be the hard part, leaving the shelter of the house to run to the barn. If she was caught out in the open . . . but she couldn't think that way. The moon was just a sliver in the Montana sky and she'd have the cover of darkness all the way. She pressed her back flat against the side of the house, said a silent prayer, and then started running.

She made it.

She had held her breath all the way, and as she entered the barn she released it, cringing at how loud it sounded. She stood stock-still for a few moments, waiting for someone to cry out her name. She held her breath again, and this time let it out slowly.

She already knew which horse she was going to take. She moved to the stall, plucked a bridle from a nail on the wall. Saddling the horse would take too long. Her intention was to slip the bridle on, and then walk the animal away until she was far enough from the house to climb astride him and then ride him bareback away from there. Riding without a saddle was no problem for her. She'd been riding since she was six, and sixteen years had made her an expert rider, saddle or no.

She'd picked the five-year-old steeldust and had been making friends with the animal for months, feeding him sugar and apples and getting him used to her touch and her smell. She held her hand out to him now so the animal could smell her, then slipped him a sugar cube to quiet him. She slid the bridle onto his head, then removed him from the stall and walked him to the back of the barn. She didn't want to take the chance of trying to take him out the front.

She opened the barn door quietly, just one of them, walked the horse out and then into the woods. She didn't bother closing the door behind her. Maybe at first they'd think the horse had wandered away by himself . . . until they checked her room.

She hoped to be long gone by then.

They'd come after her, of course. There was no way they'd allow her to just leave. She knew she was going to have to find some help. She didn't know who, though. Maybe the law, maybe not. The law could be bought. She had seen that all her life. No, maybe she'd just have to find herself a man. She was extremely pretty and well built, that wouldn't be a problem at all. And she wasn't a virgin. She'd been broke in long ago, although she was no expert at sex. She could ride and shoot much better than she could have sex with a man.

That reminded her of the gun in the sack. She took it out and tucked it into her belt. Now she had her gun, and her horse, and with each moment they were getting further from the house. Finally, when she couldn't hear the noise from the house any longer, she stopped long enough to spring onto the back of the steeldust, which she'd come to call "Baby." She hadn't meant for it to be a name, she'd just started calling him that when she was petting him and feeding him. He started to respond to it, and finally it became his name.

She settled herself onto the animal's back, tied her sack to her waist with a piece of string she took from inside. With no saddle to tie it to, she wanted to avoid having to carry it so she could keep her hands free.

"Okay, Baby," she said, leaning forward so she could speak into one of the horse's ears, "let's go."

Beau Davis moved down the hall quietly, not wanting anyone to know what he was doing. He paused outside Jill's room and listened to the sounds of the other men playing poker. He didn't play poker, mainly because he was so bad at it. There was other stuff he was better at, like drinking and bedding a woman, which was what he had in mind at the moment. He had a bottle of whiskey in his hand, and he knew Jill would be on the other side of the door.

He decided not to knock, because somebody might hear him. Since the door locked on the outside he'd have no problem getting in. He unlocked the door, opened it, and slid inside. It was dark, so she was probably in bed, asleep. That suited him just fine. He closed the door behind him, moved to the bed, and got on it . . . only to find it empty.

"What the hell—"

He jumped off the bed.

"Jill! You in here somewheres?"

No answer.

"Jill?"

Still no answer.

"Oh, shit," he said, plucking a match from his pocket and using it to light a nearby lamp. In the yellow glow of the lamp he could see that the room was empty. When he noticed the open window he knew what had happened. Now he had a decision to make. If he went and told Roy that Jill was gone, Roy would want to know what he was doing here in the first place.

If he waited until morning and let somebody else find out she was gone, maybe he'd get blamed anyway, just because he was the youngest.

He moved his weight nervously from one foot to the other, trying to decide what to do. He decided to uncork the bottle and drink a bit of it to help his thinking. He sat on the bed and started taking swig after swig from the bottle, until he ended up curled up on the bed with the empty bottle held close to his body, snoring quietly.

That's where Roy Davis found him the next morning, when he came in to wake Jill.

ONE

Five days later...

Clint saw the girl first. She had a distinct riding style, and he noticed that she was riding bareback. She was driving the horse, too, a handsome steeldust who was giving her his all.

Then he saw the riders behind her, and he knew why she was punishing the horse.

There were four of them, all men. He found it odd that while they all had their guns out—some rifles, some pistols—none of them were firing any shots at her.

All of the riders were heading straight for him.

Jill saw the man on the black horse ahead of her and decided that he wasn't with the men who were after her. She liked the way he sat his horse, and she thought that maybe he was a man who would help her.

Or maybe she would just succeed in getting him killed.

•   •   •

Clint stood his ground as the woman came riding toward him. It was obvious that the men were chasing her, yet no one had fired yet. Perhaps they wanted her alive.

"Help!" she cried out as she approached him. He noticed that the steeldust was lathered, indicating that she had been riding him hard for some time.

She reined the animal in so hard that he tossed his head. A lesser rider would have been thrown, but she sat him well, even bareback.

"You have to help me."

"What is it?"

She turned to look behind her, then back at him. She was about twenty-two, with long blond hair, and a good body packed into jeans and a buckskin shirt. In her agitated state her nostrils were flaring, her face was flushed, and she was quite striking.

"Those men are after me."

"Why?"

"I . . . don't know."

Just enough hesitation there to show that she was not telling the truth. That didn't matter, though. The four pursuers were quickly approaching.

"Get behind me," he said. "We'll talk later."

She moved her horse around behind him and his horse Duke as the men reached them.

The four men reined in their horses, exchanged a couple of glances, then looked at Clint.

"You're in our way, friend," one of them said.

"What's this about?" Clint asked.

"None of your business," the same man said, obviously the spokesman. He was thickset, probably stood under six feet when he wasn't on a horse, but he had wide shoulders and a deep chest. A powerful man. He had a pistol in his hand, but he didn't hold it like he knew how to use it.

Of the other three men only one concerned Clint. He was tall, slender, in his twenties, with a quiet, intelligent look about him. He was also holding a pistol, but in his hand it looked dangerous. The other two men, in their thirties and unremarkable-looking, were holding rifles. The look in their eyes was that of men waiting to be told what to do.

"Four men chasing a slip of a girl," Clint said. "That seems like a bit of overkill to me. What about you?"

"What—kill?" the man asked.

"It's a little too much, if you see what I mean," Clint continued.

"Look, mister," the man said, "we got to take this girl back with us."

"Not until she and I have talked some."

"About what?"

"About why four men with guns are chasing her. I think you boys ought to put up your weapons and ride off. You'll talk to this girl another day."

"Or not at all!" she said from behind him.

The spokesman glared at Clint, his hand tightening and loosening on the gun in his hand. The two men with rifles were waiting for the word. The tension in the air was as sharp as campfire smoke, tickling Clint's nose. He watched the fourth man, who suddenly rode forward, leaned over, and said something into the spokesman's ear.

The voice of reason.

"Okay," the first man said, "we'll pull back and you can talk to her, but we'll be back for her."

"That's a good plan," Clint said. "Back off and nobody gets hurt."

"We're four against one, ya know," the man said.

"Those odds don't bother me, friend," Clint said. "That gun in your hand might as well be a shovel, and these two with the rifles are real nervous. Listen to your other friend there and back off."

The two men with the rifles looked at each other and licked their lips. Because Clint showed no nervousness, theirs increased.

The fourth man put his hand on the first man's arm, a gesture of warning. Clint was starting to wonder who was in authority after all.

"All right," the first man said grudgingly, "all right . . . but mark my words, she's ours, and so's the price on her head. You'll not have either."

So that was it. Bounty hunters. What had this young woman done to bring four bounty hunters down on her?

"I haven't done anything," she shouted at them. "You've made a mistake."

"You made the first mistake, missy," the first man said, then looked at Clint and added, "and now you've made the second."

"What's your name?" Clint asked the fourth man.

"Me?" the first one asked, but Clint ignored him and kept looking at the younger of the four.

"Foreman," he said.

With that, the four men withdrew, but they didn't go very far.

TWO

As the men rode off, Clint turned the name over in his mind. The name Foreman didn't mean much to him, but the man was young. Maybe he was just making a name for himself, or maybe—which seemed more likely—he just kept to himself.

"Shouldn't we be running?" she asked.

"Before we've made our introductions?" he said. "That would be rude. My name's Clint, what's yours?"

"Jill."

He waited, then said, "Just Jill?"

She stuck her chin out and asked, "Just Clint?"

Clint smiled.

"Touché."

"What?"

"You have a point," he said. "All right, then, first names only for a while. Come on, let's ride."

"All right—"

He grabbed the reins from her before she could get into her horse.

"Let's take it easy on this animal, if you want him to live another day."

"But . . . those men."

"They won't come after us for a while."

"Why not?"

"They have to talk it over first to see if they want to try me."

"Why would they back away from you? From one man?"

He shrugged.

"My guess is they're scared. They don't mind chasing a woman alone, but they don't like the idea of facing up to a man."

They started their horses walking in the direction Clint had been going when he first saw her, which was southeast.

"Where are you going?" she asked.

"I'm heading for Texas."

She frowned.

"That's a long way off."

"Where are you heading?"

"I . . . don't know, really. I was just . . ."

"Running?"

She looked at him quickly.

"Well," he said, "they as much told me they were bounty hunters. Why would bounty hunters be after you, Jill?"

"I don't know."

"They said you have a price on your head."

"They're lying," she said, "or mistaken. They ain't the first ones to chase me. Maybe this explains why."

"Because you have a price on your head?"

"Because I look like somebody who's got a price on her head."

"You mean there's another young woman who looks like you? That's kind of hard to believe."

"Why?" she asked belligerently.

"Because it's hard to believe there's another woman as pretty as you."

She stared at him, as if trying to decide if he was serious or not.

"You want to tell me about it?"

"About what?" she asked.

"About what you're running from."

"I don't have a price on my head." She was insistent.

"I didn't say that," he said. "I just asked if you wanted to tell me why you're running."

She thought it over for a few moments.

"A man."

It was the easiest of answers.

"Naturally," he said.

She turned to look behind them.

"They're following."

"They will, for a while."

"And then what?"

"And then they'll make up their minds about what they want to do."

"And what do we do until then?"

"Well, that depends on you, I guess."

"On me?"

"I told you where I'm going," Clint said. "Do you want to ride along with me for a while?"

"What would you want to let me do that?"

He smiled.

"Nothing. As a matter of fact, I'd like the company—you know, somebody to talk to."

"Just talk?"

"That's right," he said. "Just talk."

"I probably won't go all the way to Texas with you."

"That's fine," he said. "You can ride with me as long as you want."

"What about . . . them?"

"I'll protect you from them."

"If they think there's a price of my head, somebody else might, too."

"I'll protect you from them, too."

"Why?"

"Because if I don't," he said. "who will?"

"But why would you want to do that?" she asked. "It's dangerous. There's four of them."

"Only one of them is worrisome," he said. "Look, Jill, I'm offering you my protection. I think I can protect you better than you can protect yourself."

"I can shoot," she said, leaning back to show him the pistol in her belt, "but there was too many of them. I decided to run."

"That was a good decision."

"I wasn't afraid."

"I didn't think you were."

They rode in silence for a while, and then she said, "Well, okay."

"Okay . . . what?"

"Okay, I'll ride with you for a while . . . if you want me to."

He smiled. If he wanted her to, like she was doing him a big favor.

"Thanks, Jill," he said, "I really appreciate that."

THREE

Clint was taking a southeasterly route back to Texas that would take him through Wyoming, Colorado, and a small piece of Oklahoma before finally reaching Texas. At a leisurely pace, with stopovers, he was looking for the trip to take the better part of six weeks. There were any number of friends he could stop and see along the way, but those were not the kinds of stopovers he was thinking of. He was simply thinking of sleeping in a hotel bed once in a while, having a hot meal, maybe playing a hand of poker now and again.

Now, however, he had company, at least for part of the trip.

He had no idea how long Jill No-Last-Name would be with him, but in helping her—and he'd insisted on it, hadn't he—he realized he had once again dealt himself into someone else's hand. Uninvited? Not totally. She had, after all, asked him for help that afternoon, but he knew he could have stood those men off and given her some breathing room and sent her on her way—but could he really? How long would she last

out there with bounty hunters on her trail? How long
had she lasted already? He had no way of knowing if
there actually was a price on her head, and if there
was, how long it had been there.

Unless he asked her.

"Adams," he said.

"What?"

They had camped for the night and were sitting
across the fire from each other. He had cooked up
some bacon and beans, and made a pot of coffee. He
hadn't bothered asking her to do it. He didn't want her
thinking he assumed she would because she was a
woman. It seemed like something that would have set
her off.

He had instructed her not to look into the fire, so as
not to destroy her night vision. She told him she
wasn't a fool, but he noticed that since he'd told her
not to look into the flames she was sorely tempted to
do just that. It was funny how tempted people were
by things they were told not to do, or things they were
told they couldn't have.

"Adams," he said again, "my last name's Adams."

She hesitated a moment, then said, "Church."

"Jill Church," he repeated. "That's pretty."

"But you won't see it on no paper," she said.

"I didn't think I would," he said, "and I don't recognize it otherwise, so I guess you don't have a big
reputation of any kind."

She made a rude sound with her mouth and said,
"For what, stupidity?"

Once again it sounded as if her trouble really was a man. What if the man in question didn't like losing her and had put a price on her head himself?

"The man you're running from—"

"I didn't say I was running from a man."

"Yes, you did."

She frowned. He could see that she was trying to remember if she had actually said it.

"I tell you what," he said, "*if* you were running from a man, would he have offered money to get you back?"

Now she tried to decide if he was trying to trick her somehow.

"I thought you weren't interested in a price—I mean, *if* there was a price on my head."

"I'm not interested," he said. "I don't hunt bounty."

"Then why you askin'?"

"Because if this man did offer money for your return, it means that those men—or whoever else we come across—will be trying to take you alive. Knowing that would make them easier to handle. Do you see?"

"Yeah," she said, "I see."

He waited a few moments, and when she offered nothing in return he said, "Well?"

"Well what?"

"If there was a man after you, would he offer money for you?"

She hesitated a moment, then said, "Probably."

That would explain why the men hadn't been shooting at her.

"You better get some sleep," he said. "I'll stand watch."

"You can't stay awake all night," she said. "Let's split the watch."

He hesitated.

"I can do it," she said. "I know how to stand watch."

Well, he figured, it was her they were after, wasn't it?

"All right," he said. "You want to go first or last?"

"I'll go first," she said.

"Wake me in four hours, then. I want to get an early start. We can be out of Montana and into Wyoming before midday."

He rolled himself up in his blanket and used his saddle for his head.

"I'll make breakfast in the morning," she said, just as he was drifting off.

"Fine."

"I can cook, you know."

"I guess I'll find out in the morning, won't I?" he asked.

FOUR

Clint shook Jill awake at first light.

"Didn't you say something about making breakfast?" he asked.

She grumbled and sat up.

"There was somethin' I forgot to mention," she said.

"What's that?"

"I'm real unpleasant in the morning."

"Well," he said, "we don't have to talk while you're making breakfast."

She muttered, tried to get out of her blanket and found herself tangled up in it, which did nothing to improve her foul morning mood.

She had awakened him after four hours sleep, hardly able to keep her eyes open.

"I didn't see nothin'," she had said, falling into her blanket.

"I guess they're not going to try anything tonight," Clint had said, but she was already asleep.

She had made a pot of coffee before going to sleep, but it was so bad Clint dumped it out and made another. He hoped her breakfast was better than her coffee had been. If it wasn't, then he was going to be doing most of the cooking.

He checked on the horses while she got breakfast going. If anyone had tried to make off with Duke during the night, the big black gelding would have kicked up a hell of a fuss. Clint didn't know how the steeldust would have reacted. He checked the animal for soundness and found him sturdy enough. If she had ridden him a few more hours the way she had been, though, the horse probably would have gone lame—or had a heart attack.

"We'll go easy for a few more days, boy," he said, patting the steeldust's neck. He reminded himself to ask Jill if the horse had a name—but not until after breakfast, when her foul mood lightened some . . . he hoped.

As it turned out Jill became considerably more civil when she had her first cup of coffee.

"I'm sorry," she said, "it's not something I can control."

"That's fine," he said. "As long as I know about it in advance I'm not going to take offense."

This morning's pot of coffee was better than the one she'd made during the night, and she'd managed not to ruin the bacon.

"Think they're still back there?" she asked.

He nodded.

"How can you tell?"

"We're downwind," he said. "I can smell them."

"Huh?"

"They had their breakfast going before we did," he said. "I could smell the coffee."

"Maybe we should travel faster today."

He shook his head.

"Your horse isn't ready for that yet. We should come to a town as soon as we cross into Wyoming. We can see about getting you a new horse—"

"Oh, no," she said, "I'm keeping Baby."

"—or we can rest him—Baby?"

"That's his name."

"You named your horse Baby?"

"What did you name yours?"

"Duke."

She frowned and looked over at the big gelding.

"Okay," she said grudgingly, "it fits him, but what's wrong with Baby?"

He hesitated a moment, then shrugged and said, "Nothing, I suppose. I guess one name's as good as another."

When they finished breakfast they cleaned up, doused the campfire, and got the horses ready.

"Do you have any money?" he asked her.

"Some. Why?"

"I think you need a saddle if you're going to ride much further."

"Oh," she said, "I don't have enough money for that."

"Well, we'll see what we can do about it."

He saddled Duke and boosted Jill up onto Baby's back before mounting himself.

"Think they're ready?" she asked, looking behind them.

"I think they've been ready for a while," he said. "Let's go. We'll keep a slow but steady pace. I want to make Wyoming by midday."

FIVE

They did indeed make Wyoming by midday, and the four men were right behind them.

"We gotta do something," one of them said. His name was Hy Willis.

"What would you suggest?" Foreman asked.

"We gotta take her from him."

"Yeah," Ben Munch said, "that's what we got to do."

Foreman looked at Guy Collins, who had been the spokesman when they encountered Clint Adams.

"What do you think, Guy?"

"We can't just follow them forever," Collins said. "We'll have to do something sooner or later."

"I'll bet none of the three of you recognized that fella," Foreman said.

"I don't know him," Willis said.

"Me neither," Munch said.

Collins looked at Foreman.

"And I'll bet you did."

"Yep."

There was a long moment of silence among the four men.

"Well?" Collins finally asked. "You gonna tell us?"

"Ever hear of Clint Adams?"

Now the silence was a stunned one.

"No," Willis said.

"Are you sayin'—" Munch started, but Collins cut him off.

"The Gunsmith?"

"That's right."

"Why didn't you say somethin' before?" Collins demanded. "We been followin' him all day and you didn't say nothin'?"

Foreman shrugged.

"What's the difference?"

"The difference is," Collins said, "we coulda decided to take him and all got killed."

Foreman smiled.

"Not all of us."

Collins snorted and said, "You think you can take the Gunsmith?"

"I know I can."

"How can you be so sure?" Willis asked.

"His time has passed," Foreman said, "and I'm in my prime. It would be no contest."

"Then why don't we just ride up on them and take her?" Collins asked.

"Because," Foreman said, "she might get hit by a stray bullet. Remember, she's only worth money alive."

"Dead would be so much easier," Willis said.

"We know how you like to bring them in dead, Willis," Foreman said. "This bounty is a little different, though."

"Too different, if you ask me," Munch said.

"What do you mean?" Foreman asked.

"When we decided to go after this girl nobody said nothin' about tanglin' with the Gunsmith."

"If you want to pull out, be my guest," Foreman said. "A three-way split is better than a four-way split, anyway."

"I didn't say I wanted out," Munch said. "I want my share."

"Then just shut up and do what you're told," Foreman said.

"And what is that, Foreman?" Collins asked. "What is it that we're gonna be told?"

"Just wait," Foreman said. "The time will come. We'll just have to be ready."

"Maybe we need some help," Willis said.

"You want to split this money five ways?" Foreman asked.

"N-no, I just thought—"

"We don't need any help, Willis," Foreman said. "There's too many other people after this money as it is."

"What about them?" Munch asked. "How long do you think we'll stay ahead of Maxim and the others at this pace?"

"I don't know, Munch," Foreman said. "I guess we'll just have to wait and see, won't we?"

"Waiting has never been my strong point," Collins grumbled.

"We're just going to have to get good at it," Foreman said.

SIX

The first town they came to in Wyoming was called Great Springs—although there didn't seem to be anything especially great about it. It was small, but it had what they needed: a livery, a hotel with a dining room, and a saloon.

"I don't think we could find you a horse here if we wanted to," Clint said as they rode down the center of Great Spring's one street.

"I smell food," she said, and he heard her stomach growl.

"We can eat and get going again before it gets too late."

"Why don't we stay here?"

"It's early," he said. "We can still get some miles behind us. Besides, this town's too small to stay in. If those four behind us decide to try something, I don't know how much help the local law will be—if there's any local law."

"Well, then, let's eat," she said. "I'm starved."

"Let's go to the hotel. They'll probably have a dining room."

They reached the hotel, dismounted, and left the horses out front. As soon as they entered the lobby, they found out that this was where the smell of food was coming from.

"Can I help you?" the desk clerk said. "Would you like a room?" The man seemed so hopeful that Clint knew they didn't get many strangers in town—not to stay, at least.

"We'd just like to get something to eat."

"Oh," the man said, somewhat crestfallen. "Well, go right in, then."

"Thanks."

Clint and Jill entered the dining room and found it empty. An elderly waiter came over and asked if they'd like a table.

"Pick any one," he said, when they answered that they did.

Clint chose a corner table and sat with his back to the wall, so he could see the entrance. When Jill started to sit with her back to the entrance he stopped her.

"Sit on either side of me, but not between me and the door," he said.

She complied nervously.

"You think they'll come in here?"

"Unless there's someplace else in town to eat."

They gave the waiter their order, Clint suggesting to Jill that they simply order steaks. She nodded, and he told the waiter to bring coffee right away.

"If they come in here there might be trouble," she said.

"There's a possibility they might not even come into town, Jill," Clint said. "They may just sit outside and wait to see what we're going to do."

"I hope so."

By the time the waiter brought their lunch Clint was convinced he was right. The four men were probably waiting just outside of town. If Clint and Jill didn't ride out, then they'd assume they were going to stay the night. If that happened the four men might ride in and get rooms, or camp outside if they weren't yet ready to face Clint.

"They ain't comin'," Jill said, around a mouthful of food.

"It doesn't look like it."

"Good." She seemed to visibly relax, and she slowed her eating, so as to enjoy it more.

"When's the last time you ate a real meal?"

"Days before I met you," she said. "Maybe a week."

"That's a long time. Maybe we can get some supplies here so we can eat better on the trail."

"That sounds good. I'm getting tired of bacon and beans."

"After lunch we'll find the general store and see what they've got. Some canned fruit would be nice."

She agreed, and they ate the rest of their lunch in silence. Not that Clint didn't have any questions, but he didn't think Jill had any answers for him. Not yet, anyway. Not until she learned to trust him a little more.

They finished lunch and Clint paid. They left the hotel warily, Clint stepping out first to check the street. There was no sign of Foreman or the other three men.

"It's okay," he said, and she stepped out.

"Maybe they gave up?" she asked.

"They're bounty hunters," Clint said. "They don't give up easily."

They crossed the street and followed the directions they'd gotten from the waiter before leaving the dining room. Cross the street, turn right, can't miss it, and they didn't. They walked a block and came right to it.

They bought some canned peaches and some dry goods, some coffee, and a new shirt for Jill. She insisted on paying for it, but he told her she could give the money to him later and paid for the whole shooting match.

They left the general store with their purchases in a sack, which Clint tied to his saddle.

"Let's take a ride to the livery," he said.

"I thought you didn't think they'd have a good horse here?" she asked. "Besides, I told you I didn't want another hor—"

"I'm not looking for a horse," he said, "I'm looking for a saddle."

"For me?"

"Yes, for you."

They started walking their horses up the street.

"I don't need a saddle, Clint," she said. "I can ride just fine bareback."

"I know you can," he said, "but if you have a saddle you'll be able to carry a canteen, and some supplies, and a rifle."

"I don't have a rifle."

"We can get you one of those, too."

She stopped walking.

"Why are you spending money on me?"

He looked at her.

"Because I have it, and because there are things you need."

"And you don't expect anything in return?"

"Have I asked you for anything?"

"No."

"Then there's your answer, isn't it?" His tone hardened because her suspicions of his intentions annoyed him.

"Yes," she said, a bit contritely, "I guess it is."

"So let's go and look at a saddle."

SEVEN

"Where are they going?" Foreman asked.

Willis, who was watching the town while the other three rested, said, "They left the hotel and they're walking their horses through town."

"Probably heading for the livery," Foreman said. He was lying on his back with his hands behind his neck.

"You think they're gonna stay?" Munch asked. He was sitting on the ground across from Foreman, with Guy Collins next to him.

"I doubt it," Foreman said. "That town doesn't offer them much."

"It's got a hotel," Collins said.

"If I had that gal riding with me," Willis said, "I'd sure want to get her into a hotel bed."

"Don't even think like that," Foreman said. "We bring her back alive and untouched, or we don't get paid."

"Untouched?" Willis asked. "Anybody tell the Gunsmith that?"

"Just keep watching," Foreman said.

As it turned out, the town had a livery stable that was in a state of gross disrepair, and there was nothing on hand that they could use.

"I told you I can ride bareback just fine," Jill said as they left the livery.

"If I want to buy you a saddle," he said, "why don't you just let me?"

"Fine," she said, "buy me a saddle, but it's not gonna be here, is it?"

"No," Clint said, "that's for sure. In fact, I think it's time to leave this town, don't you?"

"Definitely."

They mounted their horses and rode out of town, heading south.

"They're ridin' out," Willis said urgently.

"Relax," Foreman said, getting to his feet, "they can't get far. She's been riding her horse hard. Adams won't let her push it too hard."

"How do you know that?" Munch asked.

"Did you see Adams's horse?"

"Sure," Munch said, "a big black gelding."

"A man with an animal like that knows horseflesh," Foreman said, mounting up. "Like I said, he won't let her push her mount for a while. That's why they been keeping such a leisurely pace all this time. Come on, mount up."

"We don't get to go into town?" Munch complained.

"What for? We've got plenty of supplies. We don't need to stop."

"A hot meal would be nice," Munch said.

"And a woman," Willis chimed in.

"You can get all the hot food and all the women you want, after we get paid," Foreman said. "Now come on, mount up!"

The other three men climbed on their horses, and the four of them rode down toward town. Foreman intended to skirt the town, since it wasn't that big to begin with. He figured Adams would wait until they reached a sizeable town before he stopped. A town like that would have a telegraph office, which was what Foreman was waiting for.

Clint and Jill topped a rise on the other side of town, and then Clint stopped and turned.

"What is it?"

"Just taking a look."

Jill turned and looked, too.

"I see them," she said, "just on the other side of town."

"Yep," Clint said. "They're coming."

"I wish they'd make up their minds what they want to do," she said. She looked at Clint. "Don't the waitin' bother you?"

"The longer they wait, the more time they've got to think about what they're going to do. One or two of them might change their minds."

"Not all?"

"No," Clint said, "that fella Foreman, he won't change his mind. He'll come after us alone, if he has to."

"How do you know that? I thought you didn't know him," she said.

"I know the type, Jill," Clint said. "I can see it in his eyes."

"Do you think he knows who you are?"

Clint looked at her. "Do you—"

"I recognized your name. I've heard of you. So, do you think he knows who you are?" she asked.

"I think so," Clint said.

"That means he told the others. Wouldn't that scare them away?"

"The others, maybe," Clint said. "Not him."

"Why not?"

"Who I am would just make it better for him," Clint said. "He's the type who likes to test himself."

"He wants your reputation?"

"It might not even be that," Clint said. "He just wants to try his hand."

"Against a legend?"

Clint winced when she said "legend."

"Against another man," he said.

"But you're not just another man, Clint."

"Sure I am," he said.

"But you're—"

Clint turned around and gave Duke a little kick in the ribs.

"Let's stop talking," he said, "and keep moving."

EIGHT

Wade Maxim frowned when there was a knock at the door. He didn't stop moving, though, and the girl beneath him continued to moan. Well, she wasn't a girl, exactly. She was more like an old whore, but she was the best this town had to offer. He looked down and saw the loose flesh at her throat, the puckered skin between her breasts, and he felt himself starting to lose interest. He closed his eyes so he could continue to fuck her without seeing these things. She was wet, and that was good, he liked it wet, and just when his dick was getting interested again there was another knock at the door.

"Ah, shit!" He withdrew and rolled away from the old whore.

"What's wrong, honey?" she asked, looking at him wide-eyed. He hadn't noticed before that she had small pouches beneath her eyes. She wasn't even a decent five-dollar whore.

"Somebody's at the door," he snapped. "Can't you hear it?"

"Honey, when you're pounding away at me like that I can't hear nothin'," she said, trying to look sexy.

"Jesus," he said, "get the door, will you?"

She shrugged, got out of bed, and padded naked to the door. From behind she looked much better. Her butt had somehow managed to remain firm, and the line of her back as it disappeared between the cheeks of her ass was nice. Yeah, she was definitely better from behind.

She opened the door, and the man who was knocking stared at her, wide-eyed. Maxim knew that at first glance she really didn't seem too bad. Standing, the wrinkles between her breasts disappeared, and her breasts themselves were full and heavy, not bad even though they were starting to sag.

Also, the man at the door, Ivan Cord, was young, and he probably hadn't seen that many women naked.

"Cord!" Maxim shouted. "What do you want?"

Reluctantly, Cord tore his eyes away from the naked whore, who leaned on the door, posing with one hand on her hip.

"Get in here!" Maxim said.

Cord stepped in. The whore, Tammie—she was way too old to be a Tammie—closed the door and walked back to the bed. Maxim was also naked, reclining on the bed. Tammie sat next to him and placed one hand on his thigh. Between his legs his dick was undecided about whether it wanted to be hard or soft. As Tammie's hand rubbed his thigh slowly, it began to harden.

"What do you want?"

Cord didn't know where to look. He was nineteen, had only ever seen two other naked women in his life, one fourteen and the other seventeen, and neither of them had breasts like this one.

On the other hand he had never seen another man naked, let alone excited, and he wasn't quite sure where to look. He didn't want to look at Maxim's hairy body, but he didn't want to insult his boss by staring at the woman.

He finally decided to look at a spot on the wall above the bed. That seemed to be the best course of action.

"Cord," Maxim said tightly. "What is it?"

"Uh, we got word on the woman, boss."

"And?"

"She's with a man."

"Why doesn't that surprise me?"

"I don't—"

"Who's the man?"

"We're not sure."

"Well, find out."

"Right, boss."

"Anything else?"

"Well, yeah . . ."

"What?"

"We know that there are four men on her trail."

"And they are?"

Cord hesitated.

"Cord," Maxim prompted.

"Foreman and his bunch."

Maxim sat up and slapped the whore's hand away from his thigh.

"That son of a bitch! He's after my bounty."

Cord wasn't sure whose bounty it was. After all, Foreman was out there trailing the girl, while Maxim and his men—including Cord—were still in the town of Oswald, Montana, just this side of the border from Wyoming.

"How close are they to her?"

"Real close," Cord said. "The word we got is they been trailing them for days."

Maxim rubbed his jaw thoughtfully.

"Where are they?"

"They're in Wyoming."

"Where?"

"They're getting pretty near a town called Dexter."

"What kind of town is it?"

"Not big, not small."

"Telegraph office?"

"Yeah."

"How many hotels?"

"Two."

"Saloons?"

"Two—three if you count one in one of the hotels."

"Get out," Maxim said. "Get to Libby and tell him to get the men ready."

Sam Libby was Wade Maxim's right hand.

"Right."

As Cord left, the whore reached for Maxim again, and he slapped her hand away again. She rolled over on the bed to wait for him, her back to the window.

Maxim got up and walked to the window, stood in plain sight naked, staring down at the street without seeing it. It was odd. Maxim was forty-eight, had been hunting bounty for the better part of twenty-five years, and he was the one over the past few years who had started using the telegraph and railroad to hunt his prey.

Foreman, on the other hand, was a throwback, a young man who simply got on his horse and hunted. Maxim had done that for too many years, and he was tired of it. Over the course of his twenty-five years he had established contacts all over the country. He used them now to his best advantage. As long as there was a telegraph line in the area, he could find anybody he wanted to find.

Like Jill Church.

Foreman had been on the hunt for about three years and was making a name for himself among other bounty hunters. Maxim couldn't afford to lose Jill Church to Foreman. If he and his men were on the girl's trail, what were they waiting for? There was a reason he hadn't closed in yet. What was it?

The man with the girl. Maybe that was it. Who was he? Maybe Foreman knew who he was, and that was why he was playing it cautiously.

Maxim looked down idly and saw that his penis was hard. He was going to have to have that taken care of before he got dressed and left town.

He turned and saw the old whore lying on the bed. Suddenly, she didn't seem so old. She was lying on her side with her back to him, and her ass was very smooth and firm-looking, real inviting.

He walked to the bed, climbed in behind her, and said, "Don't turn around. . . ."

NINE

Dexter, Wyoming, served a purpose for both Clint and Foreman. Clint, as he and Jill approached the town, saw the telegraph lines and decided to make use of them.

Since Foreman had already been looking for a telegraph office he, too, was pleased to see the wires.

"I have to ask you something," Clint said, as he and Jill were riding into town.

"What?"

"Are you wanted by the law?"

"What?"

"I said—"

"I heard you," she said, cutting him off. "What do you mean, am I wanted by the law?"

"Jill, you haven't told me why there's a price on your head. I just want to know—"

"I told you there's *not* a price on my head."

"We're playing word games," he said. "I think over the past twenty-four hours I've proven my point. I'm not after anything. I just want to help you."

"But you won't if I'm wanted by the law?"

"That's not what I said."

"Then why did you ask that?"

"Because I want to know whether or not I can talk to the sheriff in this town about Foreman and his bunch. If I mention you to the sheriff, is he going to find paper on you?"

"Paper?"

"Is he going to show me a wanted poster on you?"

She looked confused and said, "Uh, no, I don't think so—"

"You don't *think* so?"

"I don't *know*," she said. "I mean, I haven't broken any laws, if that's what you want to know."

"But there might be a poster on you?"

"It depends."

"On what?"

"On whether or not that kind of thing can be bought," she said.

Clint was quiet as they approached the town's main street.

"Yeah," he said after a few moments, "that kind of thing can be bought."

"Then you won't talk to him?"

He hesitated again, then said, "I'll talk to him, but I won't mention your name."

"Why do you have to talk to him?"

"Because I might be recognized," he said, "and then he'll come looking for me."

"Are we gonna stay the night?"

"Yes, we are," Clint said. "We'll get a couple of rooms, get a hot meal, get some sleep in a real bed.

I'll talk to the sheriff, and I've got some use for that telegraph office."

"What kind of use?"

"I want to see what I can find out about this fella Foreman. I don't know him, and I'd like to find out *something* about him."

"That's all?"

"That's all, Jill," he said. "I told you before, you can trust me."

"I—I know I can."

He looked at her.

"Do you?" he asked. "Do you really?"

"Yes."

"Does that mean you'll tell me what's going on?" he asked.

It was her turn to hesitate now.

"I'll tell you what," she said finally. "You keep your promise and buy me a saddle, and I'll tell you what's going on."

Clint nodded and said, "Fair enough."

"We can't see the town from here," Willis complained. "Why are we stopping?"

"Because I'm going into town," Foreman said, "but you fellas are not."

"What?" Munch asked.

"What's the story here, Foreman?" Collins asked. "We need some time in town."

"Not right away," Foreman said. "I'm going to ride in, use the telegraph, and see if Adams and the girl are staying. If they are, I'll come back and get the three of you, and you'll have your night in town."

"And if they're not staying?" Munch asked.

"Well," Foreman said, looking at the three of them, "if they're not staying in town, neither are we. Now, settle down and wait until I get back."

As Foreman rode off, both Munch and Willis looked over at Guy Collins.

"What happened here?" Willis asked.

"What do you mean?" Collins asked.

"I mean what the hell happened here?" Willis repeated. "When Foreman joined up with us you were in charge. When did he take over?"

Collins's left hand struck Willis in the chest, knocking him off his horse. The animal shied away, and Willis had to roll to keep from being trampled.

"What'd you do that for?" he demanded, getting up and dusting himself off.

"Never mind," Collins said. "Just get control of your horse. We're gonna make a cold camp until Foreman gets back—and don't ask me any more questions!"

TEN

Their first stop was the Dexter Hotel where Clint got them each a room. He saw Jill watching him as they checked in. He wondered what she would have said or done if he'd asked for one room.

"Why don't you go up to your room," he said, handing her the key, "and get a little rest."

"Where are you gonna go?"

"I'll take the horses over to the livery," he said, "and be right back."

"What if . . . they come while you're gone?"

"They won't make a move yet," Clint said. "They're not in town, so they don't know yet that we've taken rooms. They're professional bounty hunters, Jill. Sometimes being a professional is a bad thing and can be used against a person."

"How can that be?"

"Because they're professionals they'll be slow and careful," Clint said. "They won't move until they've checked the situation out completely. We're going to use that to our advantage to get a little rest."

"Rest for me, you mean."

"For all of us," he said, "me, you, and the horses. Look, I'll be gone fifteen minutes at the most. When I come back I'll knock—"

"You don't have to do that."

This conversation had been taking place right in front of the desk. Jill turned and addressed the desk clerk.

"Can I have a second key to my room, please?"

"Of course, miss." The desk clerk, a little man with the smoothest chin Clint had ever seen, retrieved another key from her room box and handed it to her. "Will there be anything else, miss?"

"No, thank you," she said. She handed Clint one of the keys. "Just use that when you come back."

Clint took the gesture for what it was, a show of trust. Another woman might have meant it as something else entirely, maybe an invitation, but not Jill. Not at this point, anyway.

"Okay," he said, pocketing the key, "get some rest."

As Jill went up the stairs, Clint turned and looked at the desk clerk. To the man's credit he had never once given them a second glance as Jill handed Clint the second key to her room.

"Excuse me."

"Yes, sir?"

"Who's the sheriff of this town?"

"That would be Sheriff Tyler, Andy Tyler."

"How long has he been sheriff?"

The man thought a moment, then said, "Five years or so."

"Good man?"

"He does his job," the clerk said, "that's why we keep reelecting him."

"What's your name?"

"Parker, sir."

"Well, Parker, thank you for your help."

"That's what I'm here for, sir."

Clint took some money out of his pocket, but Parker waved it away.

"It's my job to help the guests in any way I can, sir," he said.

"Thank you, Parker."

The man smiled and went back to his job, which he obviously took pride in.

To be on the safe side Foreman dismounted as soon as he entered town and left his horse at the end of the street. He walked down the main street warily, keeping his eye out for two things: Clint Adams and the telegraph office.

He spotted Clint first, coming out of the Dexter Hotel. As he watched, Clint gathered the reins of both horses and began walking to the other end of the street. It was pretty obvious that he and the girl had taken a room at the hotel.

He waited until Clint was out of sight, then stopped a man and asked him where the livery was.

"All the way down the street, make a right. Can't miss it."

That was where Clint Adams had gone, all right. Next he asked the man where the telegraph office was.

"Straight ahead two blocks, on this side. Can't miss it."

Foreman continued on without thanking the man.

"You're welcome," the man said to the air and walked the other way.

ELEVEN

Clint left the horses off at the livery with special instructions for the care and feeding of Duke.

"What about the steeldust?" the liveryman asked. He was in his fifties, short and compactly built. He took all of Clint's instructions silently, even though he looked like a man who was used to taking care of horses.

"Just take normal care of him," Clint said. "You got any saddles for sale?"

"Some, in the back. Better ones at Royce's."

"Royce?"

"He's got a store in town."

"I don't need anything new or expensive."

"That's what I got, then," the man said, "what's not new and not expensive—uh, but it ain't cheap, either." He added the last, as if he felt he'd made a tactical error.

"What about horses?" Clint asked.

"For sale?"

Clint nodded.

"Out back, I got some. Want to take a look?"

"Later," he said. "The saddle's for a woman. I think she'd like to pick it out."

"The horse for her, too?"

Clint nodded.

"I can find somethin' gentle for her—"

"No need," Clint said. "She can ride."

The man turned and looked at the two horses, then asked Clint, "The steeldust hers?"

He nodded.

"She's been ridin' bareback."

Another nod.

"I reckon she can ride, then. I'll take good care of your horses, mister. You come on back when you're ready to look at the other things."

"I'll be back."

"The names Carl Belle—with an *e*."

"Carl, my name's Clint."

They shook hands and Clint left, feeling that Duke was in capable hands.

Foreman found the telegraph office and ducked inside. It occurred to him that a man like Clint Adams might also have a use for the office, if only to check on him.

Having already composed his message in his mind, he quickly wrote it down and handed it to the key operator.

"You need a reply?" the man asked.

"Yes."

"Will you wait?"

"No," Foreman said. "I'll be at that hotel up the street, whatever the name of it is."

"Not the Dexter Hotel?"

"No."

"Okay, then," the man said. "When the reply comes in I'll run it right over, Mr. ..." he looked at the telegraph, flimsy in his hand, "... Foreman."

Foreman left the telegraph office and hurried back to take position across the street from the hotel he had seen Clint come out of. He wanted to make sure that Adams and the girl had registered before he left town to get the others. There was another, smaller hotel near where he had left his horse. If Clint Adams and the Church girl were using the Dexter Hotel, then he, Collins, and the others would make use of the other hotel.

He got into position just in time to see Clint returning to the hotel, carrying his rifle and his saddlebags, proof enough that he was checking in, or had checked in already.

Foreman left his position, walked back up the street to where he'd left his horse, and rode out of town to get the others.

As Foreman walked back up the street, Clint moved to the doorway of the hotel and peered out. He'd noticed Foreman standing across the street, trying not to be seen. He didn't know what the four men would try while in town, but he was going to have a talk with the sheriff just the same, as soon as he got settled in his room. Satisfied that Foreman was not an immediate danger, he went upstairs to do just that.

TWELVE

Clint left his gear in his room and checked out the view from his window before walking down the hall to Jill's room and letting himself in quietly.

She was asleep on the bed, fully dressed except for her boots. In repose she looked younger than twenty-two, and he wondered if she'd been lying about her age. She'd probably been lying about a lot of things, why stop at her age?

He walked to her window and saw that she had the same view, but there was a ledge outside her window. Maybe he'd change rooms with her—and maybe not. They weren't out to kill her, just take her back to who-ever had put the price on her head. For trying to help her, he was probably a target to be killed—so what else was new? He was a target every day.

He wondered if she'd tell him anything today that was true.

He walked to the bed and put his hand on her shoulder. Unlike the mornings, when she woke badly, she opened her eyes and smiled at him.

"Back already?"

"Yes."

"How long did I sleep?"

"About half an hour."

She sat up and stretched her lithe body. He couldn't help but watch.

"Are you really twenty-two?" he asked her.

"Yes," she said, "I'm really twenty-two. Why?"

"You look a lot younger when you're asleep."

"Do I?"

"Yes."

"Well, I am twenty-two," she said. "That much is true."

She was as much as admitting that she'd been lying to him.

"Are you hungry?"

She thought a moment, then said, "I'm starved."

"Let's go down to the hotel dining room," he said. "We have a lot to talk about."

"Yes," she said, pulling her boots on, "we do."

The dining room was half full and they were seated immediately. They both ordered steak for lunch, and coffee. While they were waiting for the coffee he told her about seeing Foreman across the street.

"Does he know you saw him?"

"No, I'm sure he doesn't."

"What do you think they'll do now?"

"We passed another hotel in town," he said. "My bet is they'll check in there."

"And then what?"

"And then keep an eye on us."

"For how long?"

"I don't know," Clint said. "I guess that depends on who else is after the price on your head."

She opened her mouth, and he knew she was going to protest that there was no price on her head, but she stopped herself.

"Not going to deny it?"

"No," she said, "but I can't confirm it, either."

"But you suspect it?"

"Yes."

"Who put the price on your head, Jill?"

"You wouldn't know his name if I told you," she said, "but he's rich."

"Where's he from?"

"He lives in Montana."

"And he didn't want to let you go?"

"No."

"How many men does he have working for him?"

"A lot, but I don't think he's sent any of them after me."

"Just bounty hunters, huh?"

"Why would a bounty hunter take this kind of job?" she asked. "Don't they usually want to bring back their prey dead?"

"A lot of them do, yes," Clint said. "It's just easier that way."

"So why go after me?"

"I don't know," Clint said. "Maybe it has to do with who put the money up, or maybe it has to do with the amount. Would it be a lot?"

She nodded.

"Are you worth a lot?"

"I don't think so," she said. "I don't think it's that I'm worth a lot, it's just that . . . he doesn't like to lose things."

"Possessions, you mean?"

She nodded.

"So why doesn't he come after you himself?"

"Oh, he wouldn't do that," she said. "He never leaves his . . . place. He has lots of enemies. No, he'll wait for someone to bring me back to him."

"How far do you want to go to get away from him, Jill?" he asked.

"As far as it takes."

They paused while the waiter brought their coffee.

"To Texas?"

"Yes."

"That's as far as I'm going."

"Can I go with you?"

"Sure, why not," he said. "We've come this far, haven't we?"

"Clint?"

"Yes?"

"They want me alive."

"I know."

"But you . . . they'll probably kill you if you get in their way."

"I know that, too."

"And you're still willing to help me?"

"Yes."

"Why?"

"Well," he said, "in the beginning it was just because you needed help."

"And now?"

"Now," he said, smiling, "it's because I like you."

"I like you, too," she said, "and I'm very grateful."

"I talked to the liveryman about a horse and saddle," he said. "We can go and take a look after lunch."

"Fine."

The waiter came with their food and they dug in.

"I'm not giving up Baby, though," she said, around a mouthful of steak.

He smiled and said, "No, I didn't think that you would."

THIRTEEN

Willis and Munch almost whooped and hollered as they entered town.

"This is far enough," Foreman said as they reached the hotel.

"What?" Willis asked. "This little place?"

"I told you Adams and the girl are in the bigger hotel," Foreman said. "We're stayin' here."

"What's the difference?" Munch asked Willis. "It's the whorehouse we're interested in."

"And the saloons," Willis said.

"Why don't the two of you take the horses to the livery," Foreman said to them, "and then you can do what you want."

"Whatever we want?"

"Well," Foreman said, "don't get arrested, and don't get into a confrontation with Adams. Beyond that, have fun."

"Let's go," Willis said to Munch. "The quicker we get these animals taken care of, the quicker *we* get taken care of."

Foreman and Collins gave up their horses to the other two men and watched as they led them away.

"What will they do if they cross paths with Adams?" Foreman asked.

"Why didn't you ask them?"

"I'm asking you, Guy."

Collins shrugged.

"They won't do anything," he said. "Not without you, or me."

"Not without me, Guy," Foreman said. "Let's try to make sure of that, okay?"

"Sure, Foreman," Collins said, remembering what Willis had asked him, "sure."

When *had* Foreman taken over? Collins couldn't remember an exact time or place.

"Something wrong, Guy?"

"No," Collins said, "nothin'. Come on, let's get checked in."

After lunch Clint said, "I have to go and check in with the sheriff."

"What should I do?"

"Wait in my room."

"Your roo—hey, wait—"

"If they do come looking for you," he said, "it'll be in your room. Just wait in mine, and keep your gun handy."

"I thought you said you didn't expect them to try anything yet."

"Better to be safe," he said. "Come on, you go to my room"—he pressed the key into her hand—"and I'll be back as soon as I've talked to the local law."

FOURTEEN

The Dexter sheriff's office was much like any other—except for the sheriff.

First of all, this was the biggest man Clint Adams had ever seen—even seated.

Secondly, when the man stood up to shake hands he wasn't wearing a gun, and there were no guns in the office. Even the rifle rack on the wall was empty.

"I appreciate you coming in to see me, Mr. Adams," Sheriff Tyler said.

He had red hair, and the biggest ears Clint had ever seen. They weren't only large, they were prominent, sticking out from the man's head like wings.

"You're looking around the office for guns," the man said.

"Well, frankly, yes."

"I don't use 'em."

"Bear River Tom Smith tried that back in Abilene, Sheriff, and it didn't work."

"That was a long time ago, Mr. Adams," Tyler said, "and this ain't Abilene . . . and I ain't Bear River Tom Smith. Also, I been sheriff of Dexter for five years, so it's workin' pretty good so far.''

Clint suspected that the sheer size of the man—six nine standing, if he was an inch—was preventing him from guessing his age.

"Twenty-five," Tyler said, as if reading Clint's mind.

"How did you—"

"It's what everybody wonders," Tyler said. "I know, I look closer to forty, but I'm twenty-five."

"How can that be?"

Tyler shrugged.

"I think I'm just agin' faster than most people do," he said. "Maybe it's my line of work."

Tyler sat back down behind his desk in a wooden chair that looked homemade—probably specially made for his size and girth. Not that he was fat, he was just big. His hands were big, his feet, even his lips—and his torso. Oddly, his legs looked too thin to be his, too skinny to support the rest of him.

"Now, Mr. Adams, what can I do for you?"

Clint couldn't help wondering if there was a horse in town that would be able to support the man's weight. He thought Duke might be able to do it, but he couldn't think of any other animal he'd ever seen, short of a camel.

"Mr. Adams?"

"Oh, sorry," Clint said, embarrassed. "I, uh, just wanted to let you know I was in town, Sheriff, and that there seem to be four men trailing me."

"Four men? Outlaws?"

"No."

"Lawmen, then?"

"Not exactly."

"Ah," Tyler said, "bounty hunters."

"Right."

"I don't recall there being a poster out on you," Tyler said.

"There's not."

"Then why are they after you?"

"I don't know."

"Would you like me to ask them?"

"No," Clint said, "no, that's not why I came to you, Sheriff. I just wanted you to be aware of the situation in case anything . . . happens."

"Like what?"

Clint stared at the man a moment, to see if he was serious.

"Well . . . gunplay, mainly."

"If there's any gunplay in my town, Mr. Adams, I won't take kindly to it."

"Well, it won't be my doing, Sheriff, I can assure you."

"It'll be your fault and the fault of the men shooting at you," Tyler said. "I'd have to arrest whoever was left standing."

"Well, then," Clint said, "I'll consider myself warned."

Just for a moment Clint worried that the man might ask for his gun. He didn't know how he would keep the sheriff from taking it, short of shooting him—not that he would have done that, even if he thought it would do any good. He found himself wondering if a normal handgun could take this giant lawman down.

"So," Clint said, "you've been sheriff since you were twenty?"

"Nobody else wanted the job," Tyler said, "and it seemed to be something to do where I could put my size to good use."

"I bet you'd be a hell of a blacksmith," Clint said.

"We have a blacksmith," Tyler said seriously.

"Oh."

Clint got up.

"Well, it was a pleasure to meet you, Sheriff."

The sheriff stood up and extended his hand. Clint's got lost in his. If the man had squeezed, Clint doubted he'd have ever been able to fire a gun again with that hand.

"Please try to avoid trouble while you're in Dexter, Mr. Adams."

"Sheriff," Clint said, "you have my solemn word that I'll try my best."

FIFTEEN

Foreman was having second thoughts about letting Willis and Munch walk around town unattended. If they had a few beers and ran into Clint Adams, who knew what they'd do?

They had gotten two rooms, and Foreman was sharing his with Collins.

Collins, watching Foreman, could almost read his mind.

"Forget it."

"Forget what?" Foreman asked.

"Willis and Munch are not gonna brave Adams," Collins said. "They don't have the nerve. They're just gonna find themselves a couple of whores—which doesn't sound like a bad idea to me. You interested?"

"In a whore? No. I am interested in a drink, though."

"You can usually get those two things in the same places," Collins said.

"I think I'll just settle for the drink."

"Don't you like women, Foreman?"

Foreman fixed Collins with a hard stare.

"I like clean women, Collins, the kind I won't get a dose from."

"There's no guarantee you won't get a dose from a woman who's not a whore. As a matter of fact, I never knew a woman who wasn't a whore at one time or another during her life."

"Didn't you have a mother?" Foreman asked.

"Yeah," Collins said, "and she was a whore."

"Well," Foreman said, "mine wasn't."

There was a moment of silence then, which Collins wasn't sure he wanted to be the one to break.

"You go ahead," Foreman finally said, "I'll be along later. I'm gonna check on Adams and the girl, make sure they're registered, see where they're spending their time. If you see Munch and Willis, set up a schedule with them. One of us should be watching their hotel at all times starting tonight."

"Why?"

"They might try to leave while it's dark," Foreman said. "We don't want to lose them, do we?"

Collins sighed.

"I'll set it up with them."

"Good."

"See you later," Collins said.

After Guy Collins left, Foreman walked to the window. It overlooked an alley, so he turned and walked back to the bed. He wondered if Collins was telling the truth about his mother being a whore. Whether he was or wasn't, it wasn't something Foreman liked hearing. *His* mother was a saint, and he didn't think anyone should speak badly about their mother.

And whores! They were filthy sluts and he'd have nothing to do with them. He was twenty-eight and had never been with a woman he wouldn't bring home to introduce to his mother.

He didn't even know why he was associating with the likes of Willis and Munch. Every town they stopped in, they went looking for whores. He was surprised one or both hadn't died already. Now Collins, too, was going whoring. After this job, maybe he'd go and look for partners he could respect.

One thing he really wanted, though, was a cold drink and a meal. He left the room to find a place to eat. Collins had known Willis and Munch longer than he had, and if he didn't think they had the nerve to face Adams, he was probably right.

SIXTEEN

Clint entered his room and found Jill looking out the window.

"I was looking for you," she said. She was holding her gun in her hand.

"What's that for?"

She looked down at the weapon.

"I was just a little nervous."

Clint walked up to her and took the gun from her.

"Don't even pick this up unless you're ready to use it," he said. "Tuck it into your belt."

She took it back and put it in her belt.

"What are you nervous about?"

"There's four men in this town who want to harm me," she said. "I didn't know where you were."

"I told you I went to the sheriff's office."

"What happened there?"

He told her about his conversation with the man, and then described him to her.

"He sounds like a monster," she said, eyes wide.

"He's the biggest man I've ever seen," Clint said.

"He made me feel like I was in a closet. And he's got this thing about guns."

"What about them?"

"He doesn't like them."

"A lawman without a gun?"

"It's been tried before." He told her about Bear River Tom Smith, who was the law in Abilene just before Wild Bill Hickok. "He lasted about four months."

"And then what?"

"Somebody shot him."

"What's he gonna do about those men?"

"Nothing. I didn't ask him to do anything. I just wanted him to know that if trouble started I was going to defend myself."

"So what do we do now?"

"We get some rest, we get something to eat. Oh, and I want to go to the telegraph office."

"I'm coming with you."

"I just want to send one message—"

"I'm tired of just sitting here waiting for you," she said. "This is your fault."

"What's my fault?"

"I'm used to having you around, that must be why I'm nervous being up here alone. I'm coming with you."

"All right," he said, "come on, then, but if we run into those fellas just do what I tell you to do, okay?"

"Okay."

"I'm serious, Jill."

"I am, too," she said. "You're the boss. I'll do what you say."

He looked at her for a moment and then said, "I hope you mean it."

"I do," she said. "Would I lie to you?"

"Based on past record?"

SEVENTEEN

Clint and Jill entered the telegraph office, where Foreman had been standing about an hour before.

"Who are you sending a telegram to?" she asked.

"A friend of mine named Rick Hartman," Clint said. "He lives in Labyrinth, Texas, but he's got contacts all over the country. He'll be able to tell us something about Foreman."

"Like his first name?" Jill asked.

"That would be a start."

Clint composed a short telegram, the kind Hartman was used to getting from him when he needed information. It said: A BOUNTY HUNTER NAMED FOREMAN? He signed it simply, CLINT.

"Will you be waiting for a reply?" the clerk asked.

"I'll be at the Dexter Hotel," Clint said, "at least until tomorrow morning. The answer should come in tonight." He handed the clerk some extra money. "Would you bring it over there when it comes in?"

"Sure, mister," he said, "I'll take it over. Uh, who do I ask for?"

"Adams," Clint said, "Clint Adams."

As Clint and Jill left the office, the clerk was staring after them with his mouth open. He looked down at the telegraph message in his hand, then hurried to send it. He didn't want to keep the Gunsmith waiting for his reply.

"How about a drink?" Clint asked Jill.

"Sure."

Clint looked at her.

"Have you ever had a drink before?"

"Of course," she said. "I'm not a child, Clint."

"I know," he said. "You're twenty-two."

"That's right. I'd love a drink."

"Okay," he said. "Our hotel has a bar. We'll go there."

"You don't think we'll run into . . . them there?"

"We might," Clint said, "or they might do their drinking in one of the saloons."

Clint also figured that after so many days on the trail one or two—or more—of the men might also check out the local cathouse.

"Come on," he said, "we'll get a drink, and a table, and relax for a while."

"And if they come in?"

"We'll stay relaxed," he said.

"I think that'll be easier for you than me."

"I won't let anything happen to you, Jill."

She gave him a long look and said, "I'm counting on that, Clint."

EIGHTEEN

Foreman was on his way to one of the saloons when he decided to try the Dexter Hotel. A hotel that size probably had its own saloon. Maybe he'd run into Clint Adams there. It would be interesting to have a talk with the man. Interesting? Fascinating, would be more like it.

Getting to know the man you knew you were going to kill was exciting—but he'd never before gotten to know a man like Clint Adams.

The others thought that Adams was having the Church girl, but Foreman knew better. Clint Adams would no more have that girl than he would have a whore—and he'd never speak badly of his mother.

It was too bad Foreman had to kill Adams—he would make the perfect partner.

He *would* make the perfect partner, and Foreman's ego was not so large that he would not admit that he might even learn something from the man.

It was something to consider.

• • •

Maxim looked at Sam Libby as he entered the saloon. Ivan Cord came walking in behind him. Libby was in his thirties, and was not only Maxim's right hand, but his protégé, as well. Libby was a contemporary of Foreman's, although he was about five years older than the man. He was still closer to Foreman's age than he was to Maxim's.

"What have we got?" Maxim asked.

"They're in Dexter," Libby said.

He was tall, well-built, the kind of man women loved and men envied. He was handsome, good with a gun, and smart—smarter, Maxim admitted, than he was. All he lacked was leadership ability. He'd have that in a matter of years, maybe months, and then he wouldn't need Maxim anymore.

"Have you got a map?"

Libby nodded and took one from inside his shirt. He spread it on the table. Cord leaned in to have a look, as well.

"Where can they go from Dexter?" Maxim asked.

"Our information is that they've been heading south," Libby said. "If they keep on that course they'll cross into Colorado here."

"What if they don't keep heading south?" Cord asked. "What if they head east or west, or north?"

"They won't go north," Libby said, without looking at the younger man.

"Why not?"

"Because that's where they came from."

"Oh." Cord felt embarrassed and tried to save face. "What about east or west?"

"East is a possibility," Libby said. "We can have men here"—he touched his finger to the map—"in case they do."

"And west?" This time Maxim asked.

"I don't think they'll go west, Wade," Libby said. "That's too close to where the girl came from."

"Okay," Maxim said, "then it's southeast."

"Right."

"Where do you suggest?"

"I think they're heading into Colorado," Libby said. "I think we should use the railroad and get ahead of them."

"What about Foreman and his men?" Cord asked. "They're on their trail."

"Foreman's waiting," Maxim said.

"I agree," Libby said.

"For what?" Cord asked.

"That we can't be sure of," Maxim said, "but we'll have to take the chance that he won't make a move until we get into place." He looked at Libby. "Any word on who the man she's with is?"

"Yes," Libby said, folding up the map.

"Who?"

"You're not gonna like this."

"Tell me."

"We think it's Clint Adams."

Maxim thought a moment, then started laughing. He laughed so hard he slapped his knee.

"He's the Gunsmith," Cord said helpfully.

"I know . . . that," Maxim wheezed.

Cord looked at Libby helplessly. Libby simply waited for Maxim to stop laughing.

"Then what's so funny?" Cord asked.

Maxim stopped laughing and caught his breath.

"Get the men ready, Sam. Where's the nearest rail-head?"

"Two hours away."

"Okay," Maxim said, "we'll leave in half an hour."

"Okay." Libby looked at Cord. "Let's go."

As they took their leave, Maxim sat down, thought a moment, then started laughing again, shaking his head at the same time.

On the way out Cord said, "I still don't know what's so funny."

"I don't either," Libby said honestly. "Wade just figures that Foreman hasn't made a move yet because she's with Clint Adams."

"And that's funny?"

Libby shrugged.

"I guess he thinks it is."

"But isn't it bad news that she's traveling with Adams?" Cord asked. "That will make her harder to take."

"Harder for Foreman, too," Libby said. "It'll keep him away from her until we can catch up to them."

"Oh," Cord said, "but I still don't understand—"

"Cord."

"What?"

"You don't have to understand," Sam Libby said, "you just have to do what you're told."

"Right, right," Cord said, "but, uh, Sam?"

"What?"

"Can I ask one more question?"

Libby sighed, but how else was the kid going to learn?

"Go ahead."

"Can Wade take Clint Adams?"

"No."

"Can Foreman?"

"I don't think so."

"Do we have anyone who will be able to take him when we catch up to them?"

"Yes."

"Who?"

Libby stopped walking and looked at Cord.

"Me. Any more questions?"

Cord looked away.

"No."

NINETEEN

Clint and Jill were sitting at a rear table with a beer in front of each of them when Foreman walked in. They still did not have their reply from Rick Hartman, so they still didn't know his first name.

They watched as Foreman walked to the bar for a beer, and then watched in surprise as he walked toward their table.

"What do we do?" Jill said, with panic in her tone.

"Relax," Clint said. "He's alone. He just wants to talk."

"I don't want to talk to *him*."

"That's good," Clint said. "You stay quiet and I'll do the talking."

"Deal."

As Foreman reached their table he smiled.

"Mind if I join you?"

"For what reason?"

Foreman spread his arms, almost spilling his beer in the process.

"Just a talk."

"Sure," Clint said, "sit."

Foreman sat across from Clint, with Jill on his right.

"You are a lot prettier up close, my dear," he said.

Jill ignored him, and he chuckled and looked at Clint.

"It's a pleasure to meet you, Mr. Adams."

"We met before," Clint reminded him.

"Oh, that was a chance meeting," Foreman said. "This is more formal. You are Clint Adams?"

"I am."

"I thought I recognized you," Foreman said. "I saw you kill a man once."

"Killing a man is not one of my better moments."

"On the contrary," Foreman said, "you gave the man every chance to back out. It was his choice, and you killed him cleanly."

"Where was this?"

"That I don't remember, I'm afraid."

Clint leaned forward, just to see what the younger man would do. To his credit, he didn't flinch. He sincerely was not in awe, nor was he afraid, of Clint's reputation.

"What's on your mind, Foreman?"

"A partnership, actually."

"In hunting bounty?"

Foreman nodded.

"And would the first one be the price on Miss Church's head?"

"Exactly."

"What about your current partners?"

"Vile men," Foreman said. "Unsavory. Together we can cut them out."

"And then continue to be partners?"

Again, Foreman nodded.

"Together we'd be formidable."

"How do I know that?"

"Excuse me?"

"I mean, you know who I am, you know my reputation. What do I know about you?"

Foreman stared at Clint for a few moments.

"If I read you right, Clint—can I call you Clint?— you're the kind of man who would have already made use of the telegraph office to check me out. Has your reply come in yet?"

"No," Clint said without hesitation, "not yet."

"Ah, then I won't spoil it. Why don't you check out your reply and then you can give your answer to me."

"That won't be necessary. The answer is no."

"Working with me would be very lucrative for you."

"No."

"Together we could—"

"No."

Foreman frowned.

"And why not?"

"I don't hunt bounty," Clint said. "It's something I don't do."

"Have you ever done it?"

"No."

"Maybe if you tried—"

"No."

"You're not making this conversation very pleasant for me."

"Too bad."

"Consider the alternative."

"There are many alternatives."

Foreman shook his head.

"I think you know there is only one."

"And that is?"

"I'll have to kill you and take the girl."

"That's an option you'll explore," Clint said, "not an alternative—and you'll come up lacking—and dead."

"There are four of us."

"Foreman," Clint said, "if you had the slightest thought that you and your friends could take me you would have done it by now."

"That's not true."

"Isn't it?"

"No."

Foreman looked at Jill, who was studying him solemnly.

"It isn't," he said to her, then looked at Clint.

"She's in the way. Step out into the street and leave her here."

"Now?"

Foreman shrugged.

"Or at a time of your choosing."

"I see."

"Is it a deal?"

"No," Clint said, "I'm afraid I don't make deals with bounty hunters. Most of them are very untrustworthy."

"I'll give you my word—"

"I'm afraid I'd put very little value in it."

Foreman's jaw tightened. Clint saw that he had struck a nerve.

"My word is good," Foreman said. "If you're checking me out you'll find that out."

"Maybe," Clint said, "but the answer is still no."

"I came here to give you a chance—"

"And now I'm giving you one," Clint said. "Get up and walk out . . . now."

"This is not a good move on your part."

"Time will tell."

Foreman stood up. His beer stood untouched on the table.

"I hope you're not depending on the law here to help you."

"Have you met the sheriff?" Clint asked. "Or even seen him?"

"No."

"Do it," Clint said. "It's an experience you won't want to miss."

"You have an experience coming up, Adams, that you'll wish you had missed."

"I thought you were going to call me Clint."

"I'm going to call you dead," Foreman said, "and very soon . . . maybe sooner than you think."

Clint watched Foreman's eyes. He'd be able to tell if the man was going to go for his gun.

Suddenly, a man's voice said, "Is there a problem here, fellas?"

Clint's and Foreman's eyes remained locked for a moment, and then both men looked at Sheriff Andy Tyler. Clint saw the surprise in Foreman's eyes, and thought he heard a sharp intake of breath from Jill as she looked up at the lawman.

"No, Sheriff," Clint said, "there's no problem. This is Mr. Foreman, and he was just leaving. Foreman, meet Sheriff Andy Tyler."

Clint watched as Foreman looked the sheriff up and down. He knew what the man was thinking. No gun. But there was the sheriff's size to consider. How many bullets would it take to slow this man down, let alone stop him? He knew that because he'd had the same thoughts.

"Is that true, Mr. Foreman?"

"True enough, Sheriff," Foreman said. He looked at Clint. "I'll see you again, Adams."

"I'll look forward to it."

With that he turned and walked out. Jill let out a breath, and Clint wondered if she'd been holding it the whole time, or only since the sheriff walked in.

"And who is the lady, Mr. Adams?"

"This is Jill Church, Sheriff."

"Pleased to make your acquaintance, ma'am. Is there any trouble here?"

"No, Sheriff," she said, "no trouble, now that you're here."

"I'm just doin' my job, ma'am."

"And very well, too."

"Thank you."

"Would you join us for a drink, Sheriff?"

"Thanks, but no, Mr. Adams. I'm makin' my rounds, and I should probably make sure that Mr. Foreman doesn't get lost on his way back to his hotel. He is staying up the street, isn't he?"

"He's not staying here," Clint said, "so he must be."

"I think I'll just check it out." He looked at Jill and tipped his hat. "Ma'am."

"Sheriff."

They both watched the big man walk out the door.

"I think you might have a conquest there, Jill," Clint said.

"God, he's big, isn't he?"

"I told you he was."

"But I didn't think he was *that* big."

"I'll get a couple more drinks," Clint said and walked to the bar.

TWENTY

"I don't mind telling you he scares me," Jill said when Clint returned.

"The sheriff?"

"No," Jill said, "not the sheriff. Foreman."

"That's what he was trying to do."

"And I'll tell you something else."

"What's that?"

"You scare me, too."

"I just hope I made an impression on him."

"Why do I get the feeling that all you both did was scare me?"

"Come on," he said, "let's take a walk over to the livery to look at a saddle."

Willis took hold of the woman's hips and thrust himself into her from behind. She was fat, there were no two ways about it, but that was why he'd picked her. Willis liked fat whores. He liked to fuck them from behind, like this, and reach around and feel their heavy breasts hanging down. He reached around now, found this sow's breasts, and tugged on her nipples while he fucked her hard. She loved it, the little—no, big—bitch!

Willis loved it even more.

In a room down the hall Ben Munch was also enjoying a whore, but his tastes were very different from Willis's. This whore was young and slender, with almost no breasts and hips. Her buttocks were flat, like a boy's. To Munch she looked seventeen or eighteen, but what he didn't know was that this was her specialty. In reality she was thirty years old, but she made a great deal of money by pretending to be much younger. Dressed in the right clothes, she could even pass for fourteen.

Munch and the whore were belly to belly. As she looked up at him, she realized she'd never seen a face quite like his. He squeezed both his eyes shut, scrunched up his face, bit into his bottom lip, and stayed that way the whole time he was fucking her. Well, at least she didn't have to pretend she was enjoying herself by putting a look of ecstasy on her face. She wished more of the men she was with would fuck with their eyes closed.

It would make her job a whole lot easier.

Guy Collins sat in the sitting room of the whorehouse, waiting for Willis and Munch to finish their business and come on down. He knew that as soon as they had each shot their loads they'd forget women and start looking for food and drink.

"You sure you don't want one of the girls?" the madam asked again. She was grossly fat and wore so much makeup that her face looked white.

"Thanks, but no," he said. "Maybe later."

He looked around the room and it seemed to him that these whores were either too young or too old, too fat or too thin, too plain or, well, just too ugly.

Or maybe he was just comparing them all to the girl they were chasing, Jill Church.

He had not let on to any of the other three men he was riding with that he thought Jill Church was about the prettiest thing he'd ever seen. That just wouldn't do.

This bounty was fucked up from the beginning. First, they were told they had to bring the bounty back alive, then it turned out to be a woman, and then he *saw* Jill Church and felt a rush go through him like he'd never felt before.

He'd sure never felt this way about any other bounty he'd ever hunted.

Foreman left the Dexter Hotel saloon angrier than he'd been in a long time. Clint Adams had mocked him in front of the woman, and for that he was going to die. After that he'd decide if the woman was worth taking back alive. It might be worth losing the bounty just to kill her—and rape her first.

But no. Business was business. She had to be brought back alive, but nobody said she couldn't be a little bruised. She was going to have to pay for watching him eat *shit* from Clint Adams!

He walked across the street, found a cozy doorway, and settled into it. He hoped one of the others would come and relieve him soon. He needed to go to one of the other saloons and have a few drinks.

• • •

Sheriff Andy Tyler left the hotel bar thinking about Jill Church. She was probably the prettiest woman he'd ever seen. He hesitated for a few moments to think about her some more, and when he looked for Foreman he didn't see him. He frowned, knowing that he hadn't done the right thing, here. He'd let the man get out of his sight because of the way he'd reacted to a pretty woman.

Well, his mama had always told him to watch out for pretty women. He thought that maybe he should heed what his mama said.

He went to continue his rounds.

It didn't surprise Collins when both Willis and Munch came down the stairs at the same time. Those two did practically everything at the same time, and at the same speed, even fucking. Collins wondered if the two of them would end up dying together.

He met them at the bottom of the steps.

"You boys have a good time?"

They were both surprised to see him. Collins didn't usually go to the same whorehouses they did.

"What are you doin' here?" Willis asked.

"Lookin' for you two."

"What for?" Munch asked.

He told them.

"Aw shit," Willis said. "One of us has to watch that hotel all night?"

"Not all night," Collins said. "We'll take turns. Right now Foreman is over there."

"Good," Munch said, "let the son of a bitch stay there all night."

"That'll get him good and mad," Collins said.

"So what?" Willis said. "I'm sick and tired of the son of a bitch tellin' us what to do. We don't need him, Guy. Let's go back to the way it was when you was in charge."

"And how do you propose to do that?" Collins asked.

"Easy," Munch said. "We kill the asshole."

Collins considered it for a moment, then shook his head slowly.

"Boys, that'd be like killin' the goose that laid the golden eggs." It was a story he'd heard once, but neither of the other men seemed to have ever heard it.

"Huh?" Willis said.

"What goose?" Munch asked.

"Never mind," Collins said. "I think we all know that we've made more money with Foreman than we made without him."

"I don't care," Willis said. "It's not worth takin' the shit he dishes out to us."

"Maybe it is, and maybe it isn't," Collins said, "but let's put this question aside until after we collect this bounty, all right?"

"We'll talk about it after?" Willis asked.

"Sure," Collins said, "we'll talk about it."

"All right," Munch said, "let's get a drink and somethin' to eat, and then we'll flip a coin to see who goes and relieves the bastard."

• • •

Munch, who had flipped the coin, ended up losing the toss. He relieved Foreman, who told him not to take his eyes off the front of the hotel.

"If they come out and look like they're gonna leave, come and get the rest of us."

"Yeah, yeah . . ." Munch said.

"Don't fall asleep."

"I won't, Foreman."

Foreman walked back to the hotel and stopped at the front desk. He had to wake the clerk up to ask if he had a telegram.

"Huh? Oh, uh, lemme check. Uh, yeah, you got somethin'."

"Thanks."

The clerk was asleep before Foreman's foot touched the first step.

When he got to his room he saw that Guy Collins was asleep. He turned the gas lamp on the wall up just enough to read the telegram.

FOREMAN
HOLD OFF UNTIL TURNBACK CREEK, COLORADO.

It was signed with the initial "S."

He put the telegram into his shirt pocket, then removed his shirt and the rest of his clothes and got into bed. He didn't know exactly where Turnback Creek was, but he knew that Clint Adams had until they reached that town to live.

TWENTY-ONE

Clint and Jill returned to the hotel after buying her a used saddle that was serviceable and cheap. They started to go directly to the hotel dining room to have dinner, but the desk clerk called out to him.

"Sir?"

"Yes?"

"You have a telegram."

"That's what we've been waiting for," he said to Jill.

He took the telegram from the clerk and carried it into the dining room with them.

"What's it say?" she asked when they were seated.

"As concisely as Rick could put it," Clint said, "it says that Foreman has a reputation among other bounty hunters, and that he's very dangerous."

"But he's afraid of you."

"No, he's not," Clint said, "he's careful. That means he's smart, and that makes him even more dangerous."

He tucked the telegram away in his shirt pocket, and they ordered their food.

"I don't want to leave the hotel until morning," he told her later as they ate their dinner.

"Why not?"

"Just to be on the safe side."

"You think they're out there, waiting?"

"I think," Clint said, "since there are four of them, there'll probably be one of them always watching the hotel to see if we try to leave when it's dark."

"But we aren't going to do that, are we?"

"No."

"Because that would be running," she said, "and that doesn't sit right with you."

"Hey, running is fine," he said. "There are a lot of times when running is preferable to fighting."

"But this isn't one of them?"

"If we try to leave during the night," he said, "we might force them into doing something stupid."

"Like trying to stop us?"

"Exactly."

"But at least it would be over," she said. "We could stop waiting and wondering what they were going to do."

"If you wanted this to stop, Jill," Clint said, "all you'd have to do is go back. They want to take you back. If you walk out there right now, alone, all they'll do is bring you back."

"I don't *want* to go back," she said harshly, but then she softened and added, "but if I did it would save your life."

"And then you'd have to wait for your chance to run away again, wouldn't you?"

"No," she said, "I'd probably just stay—"

"Well, it's not going to come to that," he said, cutting her off.

"Why not?"

"Because you're not going back. The best thing for you to do is to just keep going forward."

"With you?"

"With me."

"No matter what?"

"No matter what."

They finished their dinner, and then Clint suggested they go to their rooms and get some sleep.

"We'll get an early start at first light."

They walked up to their rooms, and Clint waited while she unlocked her door.

"Get a good night's sleep," he said, and she nodded and started into her room.

"Clint?" she said, before the door closed.

"Yes?"

She looked at him, then looked away and said, "Nothing. I'll see you in the morning."

As he walked to his room he thought that, at that moment, she had probably come closest to telling him the whole truth.

TWENTY-TWO

Clint was just dozing off when there was a soft knock at his door. He snatched his gun from the holster on the bedpost and went to the door. He was wearing jeans, but had on no shirt, no boots, and no socks.

He opened the door a crack and looked out. Jill was standing in the hall. She was holding her gun close to her chest, in both hands, as if seeking comfort from it.

"Come inside," he said, opening the door wide.

He closed the door behind them.

"What's wrong?"

"I can't sleep."

"Why not?"

"I'm too nervous," she said. "I keep waiting for someone to kick in my door."

"Do you want me to sit outside your door all night?" he asked.

"No," she said, "that would be silly. You need to get some sleep, too."

"What, then? Want me to come and sleep in a chair in your room?"

"No," she said, "I thought maybe I could sleep in here tonight."

"Okay," Clint said, "you take the bed, I'll take that chair—"

"You can't sleep in a hard chair," she said. "I just thought we'd . . . sleep together."

Clint took a good long look at her to see if she meant what he thought she meant.

"Jill—"

"I know," she said. "I gave you a hard time about this before, but I know now that you're just helping me because you want to, and not because you want something."

"And now what do you want?"

She moved closer to him and said, "I want to feel safe."

She put her arms around him and laid her head against his chest. He could smell her hair and feel her heat through her clothes.

"Damn it, Jill," he said suddenly, holding her at arm's length, "don't play games."

"I'm not playing games, Clint," she assured him. "I—I'm not a virgin, but . . . but I'm not very experienced, either."

He pulled her to him then and kissed her. She returned the kiss avidly, raking his back with her nails, then sliding her hands between them to undo his belt.

They undressed each other, and he took her to bed. Her body was slender, but her breasts were firm and rounded, her nipples remarkably responsive to his touch. When he took them in his mouth she shivered

· and moaned, and when he kissed his way down her belly until his mouth was nestled between her legs she gasped.

"Oh, God . . . what are you . . . I've—I've *never*—" she stammered.

"Relax," he told her, "just relax. I'm going to make you feel very safe, and very relaxed."

Of course, he was going to make her feel something else entirely before that. . . .

Later she lay nestled in his arms, waiting for her breathing to return to normal.

"I guess I'm even less experienced than I thought," she said. "I've *never* felt anything like that before."

"And how do you feel now?"

"Mmm," she said, "my body feels like it's turned to liquid."

"You should be able to sleep now."

"Mmm, I am tired," she said, "but can't we do it again before we sleep?"

"Again?"

She nodded and rubbed his belly with the palm of her right hand.

"Just one more time," she said, "maybe something else different. I think I could learn a lot from you, Clint Adams."

"Uh-huh," he said, "and probably kill me in the process. I'm a lot older than you, you know, Jill."

"Oh," she said, sliding her hand even lower, "you're not that old."

"I need to rest—"

"Look," she said, touching his penis, which was responding to her touch, "is it a miracle? You don't seem to need any sleep at all."

"Jill—"

She slid atop him and began rubbing herself against him. Her breasts flattened against his chest. He reached around and cupped her buttocks, holding her to him, trapping his erect penis between them.

"Okay," he said, "one more time, and then we go to sleep, right?"

"Of course, Clint."

"Promise."

"I promise," she said, moving up so that her slick, wet cleft was rubbing against his rigid penis, "after this I won't bother you again . . . until morning. . . ."

TWENTY-THREE

She kept her word, but at first light she was down between his legs, teasing him awake with her tongue. She took him into her mouth as he woke up, and while she was enthusiastic he knew she had told the truth about being inexperienced.

Still, that didn't keep it from being a very pleasant experience.

"I know I have a lot to learn," she said as they dressed.

"Jill," he said, "you were wonderful."

"I feel so . . . different," she said, spreading her arms. "Like I'm a woman for the first time in my life."

He went to her and kissed her.

"You are one hell of a woman," he said, "but now we have to get going."

"What about them?" she asked. "Won't they be watching?"

"They'll be watching, but they're expecting us to leave today."

"I don't understand what they're waiting for."

"I think I know."

"What?"

"Come on," he said, "I'll tell you on the way."

They stopped at her room to pick up the rest of her things, then left the hotel and walked to the livery. Clint saw one of the men in the doorway across the street, but didn't pay him much mind as he stepped from the door and started running up the street, toward the town's other hotel.

"Well?" she asked. "What did you mean?"

"I think they're waiting for help," he said. "It's obvious now that they know who I am."

"Help from where?"

"Foreman probably used the telegraph, just as we did, to send a message to someone."

"But they don't have time for someone to come here and help them."

"He probably contacted someone to meet them up ahead."

"But where?"

"They're going to have to guess."

"But . . . they don't know you're heading for Texas," she said.

"But they know we're heading south."

"Maybe we should change direction, then."

"Maybe we should," he said as they approached the livery. "We'll talk about it more once we're safely away from town."

When they got to the livery he saddled the steeldust, Baby, with Jill's new saddle, then saddled Duke.

"I wonder which of these horses are theirs?" he said, looking around.

"We could find out," she said. "Then we could . . ."

"What? Hobble them? Hurt them?"

She looked at him.

"I couldn't do that," she said.

"No," he said, "I couldn't, either." Not unless their lives depended on it, and right now he didn't think that was the case.

They mounted up.

"How does it feel?"

She wiggled her butt around and said, "It feels fine. I don't mind telling you, it feels better than bareback."

"Well," he said, "at least now you can travel in a little more comfort."

"Did I say thank you for the saddle?"

"You said thank you for a lot of things last night, Jill," he said.

He was surprised when she blushed.

"You're very pretty when you turn red."

"Shut up and let's get going."

TWENTY-FOUR

Ben Munch banged on the door of the hotel room Foreman and Guy Collins were sharing until Collins opened it, bleary-eyed.

"They're leavin'," Munch said.

"When?"

"Now," he said. "They're headin' for the livery."

"How do you know they're leavin'?" Collins asked.

"Adams had his rifle and saddlebags with him."

"Okay," Foreman said from inside the room. He sounded wide awake. "Wake Willis and let's get goin'."

"Right."

Collins closed the door and turned to see that Foreman was already dressed.

"Did you go to sleep dressed?"

Foreman looked at him.

"I'm always ready, Guy," he said. "You know that."

Collins started pulling on his pants.

"When are we gonna stop followin' them and make a move?" he asked.

"Soon," Foreman said, "very soon. I sent a telegram to a friend of mine yesterday."

"What for?"

"He'll meet us further along the trail."

"How will he know where to meet us?" Collins asked. "We don't even know where we're goin'."

"We're going south," Foreman said. "My guess is Adams is headin' for Texas. Somewhere between here and there we'll take them."

"And this friend of yours?" Collins asked. "Is he in for a full share?"

"Don't worry about that," Foreman said. "That'll be between him and me."

"Who is this friend? Do I know him?"

"You know of him," Foreman said, "but I'll let it be a surprise."

"I hate surprises."

Foreman laughed.

"Finish getting dressed and let's get going."

Wade Maxim watched the countryside go by as the train picked up speed on the flats. He remembered the first time he'd ever robbed a train, as a young man, riding with the Devil's Hole gang. Those were the days.

"Wade?"

He turned to the man next to him. Sam Libby had the map spread out on a flat surface. It looked like he had borrowed some passenger's suitcase.

"This is where I figure we can intercept them, if they keep heading south."

Maxim leaned over and looked to see where Libby's finger was pointing.

"What's there?"

"A town called Turnback Creek."

"Never heard of it."

"It isn't much of a town," Libby said, "but it's there."

"And if they don't keep headin' south?"

"My guess is they will."

"Is this a strong guess, Sam?"

"As strong as they get, Wade," Libby said. "If it's Adams she's riding with, he's been spending a lot of time the past few years in Texas. I think it's his adopted home, or something."

"That's a damned fool thing for a man with his reputation to do," Maxim said. "Adopt a home."

"It works out for us, though," Libby said.

"Let's hope it does," Maxim said. "Are you ready for Adams, Sam?"

"Ready as I'll ever be."

Maxim looked at Libby for a long moment.

"Well, hell, Sam," he said finally, "I just hope that's ready enough."

TWENTY-FIVE

They entered Colorado, and by the time they left Denver and Leadville behind Clint was starting to worry. He would have thought they'd have made a move by now.

"What are you thinking?" Jill asked.

"I was just wondering about our friends."

"I was hoping you were thinking about me."

"I am," he said, "always."

Since they left Dexter they had been sharing their bedroll. Still, she had not opened up to him yet and told him the truth. He wondered what more he had to do to gain *that* much trust.

"Why are you starting to worry about them?" she asked.

"They've got too much patience," he said. "I don't like it."

"What about changing direction?"

"If we did that," Clint said, "we wouldn't be going anywhere. I don't like being aimless."

"So we just keep waiting?"

"Maybe we start to push a little," he said, "starting with the next town."

"And what's that?"

"I saw a signpost," he said. "It's called Turnback Creek."

"Have you ever been there?" she asked.

"I've never heard of it."

"What if it's a little town?"

"We'll have to take our chances. This has gone on too long. They're probably getting impatient."

"Well," she said, "if you are, I'm sure they are."

"I'm not getting impatient," Clint said. "I think I'm just getting weary."

"I know I am," she said. "I've been running for weeks now. I'd like to stop someplace and just rest— someplace where no one can find me."

"Near the water?"

"A lake?" she asked. "A river?"

"How about the ocean?"

"I've never seen the ocean."

"It's beautiful," he said. "There are beaches in California that would take your breath away."

"You think I should head for California?" she asked. "That's too close to where I ran from, Clint."

He looked at her and said, "Exactly."

"Still not saying who you contacted?" Guy Collins asked Foreman.

"No."

Collins looked behind them at Willis and Munch, who were riding in tandem a few yards behind them.

Both men were staring at Foreman's back, like they'd like to put a bullet in it.

Collins had been thinking about what the other two men had said, about killing Foreman. Since Foreman joined up with them, though, Collins had been putting money away—more money than they'd ever seen before Foreman came along. He knew that Willis and Munch spent their money faster than they made it, but that was not the case with him. In his case, killing Foreman would be the worst move he could make. That meant that if and when Willis and Munch made their move, he was going to have to side with Foreman.

Unless he just warned him ahead of time.

"What are you thinking?" Foreman asked.

"Huh? Oh, nothin'."

"Don't go wanderin' off in your head on me, Guy," Foreman said. "Things are gonna start happenin' soon."

Collins looked at him.

"How soon?"

Foreman looked behind them, satisfied himself that the other two couldn't hear him.

"Turnback Creek."

"What the hell is that?"

"It's a town in Colorado."

"Where in Colorado?"

"Not far," Foreman said. "I saw a signpost further back."

"And that's where your man is gonna be?"

"That's it."

"And who is it?"

"You'll know when we get there."

"You don't trust me."

Foreman looked at him.

"Should I trust you, Guy?"

"Why not?"

"I'll tell you why not," Foreman said. "Your friends back there are planning to kill me. Have they talked to you about it?"

"W-what?"

Foreman stared at Collins for a few moments, then smiled and shook his head.

"Yeah, they did."

"H-how did you know?"

"I can tell, Guy," Foreman said. "I can tell when a man wants to kill me. For instance, when I was talking to Clint Adams—"

"You talked to Adams?"

"I did, yeah," Foreman said, "back in Dexter."

"Why didn't you tell us?"

"Tell *them*?" Foreman asked, jerking his head back toward the two trailing riders. "Let me finish what I'm saying. I could see in Adams's eyes that he didn't want to kill me. I can see in Willis's eyes and Munch's eyes that they do. They don't like me, and they're stupid. They're too stupid to realize that they're making more money with me than they made before."

"They know it," Collins said, "they're just too stupid to care."

"But you're not stupid, Guy."

"No."

"No," Foreman said, "you've been putting money away in a bank in Laredo."

Collins gaped at Foreman.

"H-how did you know that?"

"I know everything, Guy," Foreman said. "Well, almost everything. There's still one thing I don't know."

"W-what's that?"

"I don't know who you're gonna side with," Foreman said, "them or me. Do you have enough money put away already to kill me?"

"You tell me," Collins said. "I'll bet you know how much is in my account."

"I do, Guy," Foreman said, "I do, and in my opinion, it's not enough."

Collins hesitated a few moments, and then said, "No, it's not."

"So I'll ask you again, Guy," Foreman said, "when it comes down to it, when this is all over and Willis or Munch—or both—try to kill me, whose side will you be on?"

Collins didn't answer right away.

TWENTY-SIX

Sheriff Stewart James stepped out onto the street and took a deep breath. He didn't often think of himself as the sheriff in Turnback Creek. That was because he had very little to do, usually. This week was different, though. Earlier in the week five strangers had ridden into town. Strangers in Turnback Creek were a rarity, but what was even more peculiar was that they had taken rooms in the hotel. And the strangest occurrence of all was that they were still here.

"Leave them alone," Emily James had told him. "They're not hurtin' anybody."

"But why are they here?" he'd asked his wife, just that morning at breakfast.

"Maybe they're robbers, Pa," his ten-year-old son Isaiah said.

"Hush, Isaiah," his mother had said, "they're no such thing. Don't let your imagination run away with you." Then she turned her stern gaze on her husband and said, "Neither one of you."

"My imagination is just fine, Emily. I'm just trying to do my job, is all."

"Your job is running this place," she said to him. "You're just the part-time sheriff of Turnback Creek, Stewart. Don't forget that. The folks here don't pay you enough to go pokin' into the business of five strangers. Did you hear what I said? Five?"

"I hear you, Emily," he said, getting testy himself. "I know how to count just fine."

"What are you gonna do, Papa?" his fifteen-year-old daughter Rachel asked.

"I'll just have a talk with the gentlemen, Rachel, that's all."

"You gonna take a gun, Papa?" Isaiah asked.

"Well, now, I don't think a fella needs a gun just to talk to some other fellas, do you, Son?"

"You do if they're bandits!"

"Isaiah!" Emily snapped. "What did I tell you about your imagination."

"My imagination is just fine," Isaiah said, emulating his father.

Emily glared at her husband, who simply shrugged and asked, "What did I do?"

Now Sheriff James was walking down the street toward the hotel, wondering if maybe he shouldn't have left his rifle back at the house for this little visit.

"Lawman comin'," Sam Libby said to Maxim.

"Is that a fact?"

They were in the Turnback Creek Saloon.

"He's walkin' over from the hotel," Libby said, turning away from the window to look at Maxim. "I guess he was lookin' for us there."

"I wonder what took him so long to come lookin'," Cord wondered from the bar. "We been here long enough."

"You got to remember this is a part-time sheriff," Maxim said. "That's what we heard. Hey, bartender?"

The bartender, a fat man with a red face made even redder by the fact that he was afraid of these men, turned and said, "Me?"

"Ain't that true?" Maxim asked. "Ain't your sheriff a part-time lawman?"

"That's right," the bartender said. "He's got a ranch just outside of town."

"Town this size don't need but a part-time sheriff," Cord said.

"He's comin' in," Libby said, and backed away from the window to stand at the bar.

"Should we take 'im?" Cord asked, putting his hand on his gun.

"Sam," Maxim said, "would you do me a favor and keep that young fella from doing something stupid."

Libby put his hand on Cord's arm and said, "Take your hand away from your gun, son. We're just gonna talk."

"I'm gonna talk," Maxim said. "Don't anybody else say a word."

There were only the three of them in the saloon, Maxim, Libby, and Cord. The other two men were asleep in their hotel room.

Maxim kept his eyes on the door, preparing to welcome the sheriff.

TWENTY-SEVEN

"That's it?" Jill asked.

Clint tried to hide his disappointment.

"That's Turnback Creek?"

He stared down at the collection of buildings that made up the town of Turnback Creek. If there were a dozen, there were a lot. On the outside of the town there seemed to be some homes, a couple of which might even have been called ranches, if one was in a generous mood.

"It's, uh, not much," Clint admitted.

"It's nothing!"

"Well, there's one good thing," Clint said.

"What's that?"

"It's got a telegraph office. See the poles?"

"Why would a town this size have a telegraph office?" Jill asked.

"I don't know."

"What if it's not working?"

"Well, we weren't exactly looking for a working telegraph, Jill."

"What were we looking for?"

"A place to make a stand."

Jill shook her head and said, "Last Stand at Turn-back Creek. That sounds like a bad penny dreadful."

As Sheriff James entered the saloon he noticed the two men standing at the bar, one young, one about ten years older, in his thirties. The lone man sitting at a table was his age, early forties, maybe a little older. He also noticed that Leo, the bartender, was redder in the face than usual. That usually meant that Leo was either nervous or scared.

"Not much business today, Leo," James said, walking to the bar.

"No, Stew," the man agreed, "not much."

"I'll have a beer."

"S-sure."

James knew that all three men were watching him. He tried to appear as casual as possible.

Maxim looked at Libby, who mouthed the words, "No gun." Maxim nodded.

"Thanks, Leo," James said, accepting the beer.

He turned as he was bringing it to his mouth and looked at Maxim above the rim.

"Are you Mr. Maxim?"

"That's right."

He turned and looked at the other men.

"I guess one of you would be Cord, and one would be Sam Libby."

"I'm Libby," the older one said. The younger one was standing between James and Libby.

"How do you know our names, Sheriff?"

"Oh, well, I asked at the hotel," he said. He still hadn't taken a sip of his beer. "They told me that two men were still in their rooms, and the clerk and me, well, we figured out who was who. He told me that a man named Maxim looked like the man in charge and you"—he gestured with the beer mug without spilling a drop—"look like the man in charge."

"That's right," Maxim said, "I'm in charge."

"Would you mind if I asked what you were in charge of?" he asked. "I mean, for a man to be in charge, I guess he ought to be in charge of something."

Maxim laughed and played with the mug in front of him, which was half filled with beer. He picked it up and moved it around on the table, leaving a series of intertwined wet circles behind.

"I'm in charge of my men."

"Uh-huh," James said. "Well, just what is it you and your men do?"

"We hunt, Sheriff."

"Hunt, you say."

"That's right."

"Well . . . hunt what?"

Maxim studied the man and decided to play it straight with him. He didn't look or act like a farmer or a rancher who was a part-time sheriff. The hand holding the beer was rock steady.

"Men, Sheriff," he said, "we hunt men."

"Oh," James said, "you mean you're bounty hunters."

"That's right," Maxim said. "Do you have a problem with that?"

"Me—no, no, I don't have a problem with that, no, sir," James said, shaking his head. "That's what you do for a livin', that's what you do for a livin'. Who am I to judge you?"

"That's not an attitude we usually run into with the law," Maxim said.

"Well, I might as well tell you, bein' the sheriff here in Turnback Creek is just sort of a part-time job for me."

"I noticed you don't have a badge."

"The town can't afford a badge," James said. "Folks just sort of know that I'm the sheriff."

"And couldn't they afford a gun?"

"A gun? Oh, I have a gun—a rifle, anyway. It's at my house. Makes my wife nervous to see me leave the house with a gun."

"You got a wife," Maxim said.

"Oh, yeah, I do, twenty years now."

"And kids?"

"Son and a daughter," James said.

"That's nice."

"It is, actually. Have you got kids, Mr. Maxim?"

"No," Maxim said, "no kids for me, Sheriff."

"Well, see, my kids are the reason I took the job as part-time sheriff. I want to keep this town a safe place for them. You understand that, don't you?"

"Sure, sure," Maxim said, "I understand."

"I figured you would," James said. "I'm just wonderin', Mr. Maxim, what brings you and your men to Turnback Creek. Wouldn't be that you're huntin' for one of our citizens, would it?"

"Not that I know of, Sheriff," Maxim said.

"I see. Then you and your men, you're just sort of passin' through?"

"That's right."

"Been here a few days, though."

"That's right, too. See, we're supposed to meet some friends here. When they get here, well, we'll be on our way."

"That's fine, that's fine," James said. "You wouldn't know just when your friends were gettin' here, would you?"

"Not for sure, Sheriff, no," Maxim said, "but it should be pretty soon."

"That's fine," James said again.

He turned his head and looked at the young man, Cord. The man returned his look, his eyes narrowed, his body tensed.

"This young fella seems a bit keyed up to me," he said to Maxim. "Does he seem a mite keyed up to you?"

"A mite," Maxim said, "but he's young. He'll learn to relax."

"That's good," James said, putting his beer down.

Cord looked at the beer, then at the sheriff. He couldn't keep quiet any longer.

"You ain't gonna finish your beer?"

"Naw," James said, "to tell you the truth, I don't like the stuff."

"Then why'd you order it?"

James smiled and said, "Gave me somethin' to do with my hands, son."

"Don't call me son."

"Cord," Libby cautioned.

"Why we kowtowin' to this lawman?" Cord demanded. "He ain't even got a gun."

"Son," James said, "if I needed a gun, I'd get one."

"Where?" Cord demanded.

"Well," James said, "seein' as how the closest one to me is yours, it would have to do."

"You can't take—"

Before Cord could finish, Sheriff Stew James had his gun in his hand. Cord's eyes widened. He had hardly seen the man move.

James turned the weapon over in his hands, and then handed it back.

"It needs cleanin'," he said to Cord. "You better take better care of your firearm, son."

He looked at Maxim and said, "Nice talkin' to you."

"And to you, Sheriff," Maxim said as the man went out the door, "real interestin'."

Maxim looked at Libby, who shrugged.

"It seems we might have a little somethin' more here than a part-time sheriff, huh?"

Maxim stood up and walked to the bar. Cord was just returning his gun to his holster when Maxim backhanded him across the face.

"What was that for?" Cord demanded through lips that were cut and already swelling.

"Give me your gun."

"Why?"

"Give it to me!"

Cord took out his gun and handed it to Maxim, who held it in his left hand. He drove his balled up right hand into the younger man's belly.

"Don't ever let me see you let another man take your gun!" he said to Cord tightly. He leaned over so he could speak in the doubled-up man's ear. "I ever see you let a man take your gun from you again, you won't be ridin' with us. Is that understood?"

Cord nodded, and then slid down so that he was sitting on the floor.

Maxim tossed his gun to Libby.

"Give it back to him when he stands up. I'm goin' back to the hotel. Come and get me if you see anyone."

"Sure, Wade."

Maxim walked out of the saloon. Libby tucked Cord's gun into his belt.

"I'll have a beer," he said to the bartender, then looked at the untouched one the lawman had left on the bar. "Never mind," he said, picking it up, "I'll just have this one."

TWENTY-EIGHT

Sheriff Stew James breathed a sigh of relief as he left the saloon. It had been many years since he'd been in that situation. He was proud of how he had handled it, but he wasn't proud of the fact that he was now shaking. He held his hands out in front of him and couldn't keep them still. He walked away from the saloon, hands clasped together.

Bounty hunters!

Just what he needed in Turnback Creek right now. If their leader had been telling the truth, and they were just waiting to meet someone, that was fine. If not, then he was going to have some trouble on his hands.

As he walked down the street he couldn't believe his eyes. Riding into town were two more strangers, a man and a woman. Were these the people the bounty hunters were waiting for? And if they were, were they friend or prey?

James decided that since he was bracing strangers today, he might as well continue. He shook his hands out, to try to stop them from shaking, then walked out into the middle of the street and waited for the two riders to reach him.

"What does he want?" Jill asked as they spotted the man standing in the street.

"I don't know," Clint said, "but I guess we'll find out."

When they reached the man standing in the street, they reined in their horses.

"Can we help you?" Clint asked.

"Maybe," the man said, "or maybe I can help you."

"Who are you?"

"My name is Stewart James," the man said. "I'm the sheriff of Turnback Creek."

"I don't see a badge," Jill said.

"I'm the part-time sheriff," James said. "The town can't afford a badge."

"What can we do for you, Sheriff?" Clint asked, accepting the man at his word.

"You can tell me what you're doin' in Turnback Creek, mister."

"Just passin' through."

"Lots of people seem to be passin' through."

"There are other strangers in town?" Clint asked.

"Yeah, there are. That interests you?"

"It sure does."

"Are you supposed to meet somebody here?" James asked.

"No," Clint said, "like I told you, we're just passin' through."

"What's your name, friend?" James asked.

"Clint Adams."

"The Gunsmith?" James asked without hesitation.

"That's right."

"Mr. Adams," he said, "would you like to stop at my place for some coffee and homemade peach cobbler?"

"What?"

"My wife makes the best peach cobbler."

"We *were* going to check into the hotel," Jill said.

"Maybe you just better put that off for a while, miss," James said, "and come with me to my place."

"Maybe we should do what the sheriff asks, Jill," Clint said.

"I think you'll find it to your advantage, Mr. Adams," James said.

"Lead the way, Sheriff."

As Sheriff Stewart James led Clint and Jill off the street and away from town, Wade Maxim came out of the saloon and looked up and down the street. He didn't see the sheriff anywhere, so he turned and started walking toward the hotel.

TWENTY-NINE

"Why did you bring these people here?" Emily James whispered to her husband as they stood at the stove.

"I'm trying to keep people from being killed, Emily," he replied. "It's my job. Now, bring the coffee to the table...." She gave him a hard look and he hastily added, "Please."

Emily was a hard woman when it suited her, but she was a strong woman, as well, and Stewart James not only enjoyed that strength, he counted on it—he knew that when he needed it, it would be there.

He walked to the table where Clint and Jill were sitting and sat with them. Also sitting at the table were Isaiah and Rachel.

"You're real pretty," the fifteen-year-old said to Jill.

"Well, so are you, sweetie."

"How old are you?"

"Rachel!" James said, scolding. To Jill he said, "I'm sorry."

"It's all right," Jill said.

"I only want to know how long I have to wait to be that pretty, Papa."

"I'm twenty-two, Rachel. How old are you?"

"I'm fifteen," she said, shaking her head. "I have a long time to wait."

"No, you don't, Rachel," Clint said. "You're a beautiful young girl right now."

"You really think so?" she asked, brightening, and suddenly Stewart James thought that his daughter had gotten what she'd wanted all along.

Smart girl. Maybe too smart, for her age.

"Rachel, don't you have some chores to do?" James asked his daughter.

"But, Pa," she said, "I want to talk to Cl—I mean, to Jill."

"You can talk to Jill later," the sheriff said. "Go on, now, do your chores."

"Oh, Pa," she said, shaking her head. "Will I see you later . . . Jill?"

"I'm sure you will, Rachel."

"You, too, uh, Mr. Adams?"

"Yes, Rachel," Clint said, "me, too."

"Come on, Isaiah," Rachel called.

"Pa didn't say I had to do my—"

"You go with your sister, Isaiah," James said. "There are some things I have to talk to Mr. Adams about."

"Oh, all right," Isaiah said.

After the two children left, Emily brought a pot of coffee to the table.

"I hope you like strong coffee, Mr. Adams," she said, placing the cups on the table and filling them.

As the aroma of the coffee hit his nostrils Clint knew it would be perfect.

"There's no other way to make it, ma'am," he assured her.

"Well," she said, leaving the pot on the table, "if you'll excuse me there are some chores I need to tend to, as well. Please feel free to stay to supper if it's, uh, possible."

"Thank you, Mrs. James."

"Just call me Emily, please," she said, and took her leave, as well.

"You have a lovely family," Jill said to James.

"Thank you."

"That's a good woman, Sheriff," Clint said, "if you don't mind my saying so."

"No, I don't mind at all," Stew James said. "I know she's a good woman. I think we better start talking about you two, though."

"What about us?"

"Well, there's five bounty hunters over at the hotel and saloon, waitin' on somebody," James said.

"What makes you think they're waiting for us, Sheriff?" Clint asked.

"I don't know if they're waitin' for you," James said. "They said they're waitin' on some friends, but then you come ridin' into town. That's seven strangers in one week. Too much coincidence for me."

Clint and Jill exchanged a glance, and then looked at the lawman.

"You got somethin' else to tell me?" he asked. "More bad news?"

"I think you can increase the number of strangers in your town, Sheriff, by four more."

"Come again?"

"There are four men trailing us, and they'll soon be here, as well."

"And who might they be?"

"Bounty hunters."

"More of 'em?"

"I'm afraid so."

"Which one of you's got that much of a price on your head?"

"It's not me," Clint said.

"Miss?"

She looked at the sheriff, then Clint, then back to the sheriff.

"Well, I guess it's time to fess up," she said.

"Past time, if you ask me," Clint said.

"You don't know what she's wanted for?" the sheriff asked.

"No, I'm just trying to keep her alive and well."

"Now, I wouldn't know if there's posters on you, young lady, because bein' a part-time sheriff I don't have an office. I also don't get any posters, so if there's a whopper of a price on you, you're gonna have to tell me . . . or not."

"To tell you both the truth—"

"That'll be different."

"—I don't know how much of a price there is. I can only tell you that I ran away from a man who's got a lot of influence, and lots of money."

"Well," the sheriff said, "that's usually a pretty powerful combination. Who might this rich and powerful man be?"

"Have you ever heard of Roy Davis?"

"I ain't," James said. He looked at Clint. "You?"

"The Montana Davises?" Clint asked.

She nodded.

"Which one's he?"

"He's the oldest son."

"Who are the Montana Davises?" James asked. "Somebody fill me in before we go any further."

"They're a powerful family in Montana," Clint said, "with political ties. The father, Ben, is a state senator. He's got three sons, Roy . . ." He looked at Jill for help.

"Beau and Brady. Beau's the youngest and dumbest; Roy's the oldest and smartest; Brady is the middle one, and he's big and mean."

"So you ran away from Roy?"

"Roy took it into his mind that he owned me," she said. "He started keeping me prisoner in his house. Not the big house, where his father lives, but in a smaller house that Roy built on their property."

"A prisoner?" James asked.

"Well, I wasn't chained up or anything, but I wasn't supposed to leave the house."

"But you did," James said.

She nodded.

"One night, while Roy and his friends were playing poker, I sneaked out a window. I'd finally had enough. Roy was. . . . he was going to start sharing me with his brothers, and maybe with his friends."

"That bastard," James said.

"So I lit out, and I been runnin' ever since. I was runnin' when I met Clint, and he's been helping me, even though I never told him the truth."

"Why not?" James asked.

"Well, I didn't know how far the Davis power spread," she said. "I didn't know if Clint would help me if he knew who I was running from."

"Let me get this straight," James said. "This fella Roy Davis put a bounty on your head just because you ran away from him?"

She nodded.

Stew James sat back in his chair and said, "Well, if that don't beat all. A fella puttin' a price on his girlfriend's head."

"I'm not his girlfriend!" Jill snapped.

"Beggin' your pardon, Miss Jill," James said immediately, "I guess I don't know what I'm talkin' about. I'm sorry."

"That's . . . that's all right," she said. "I guess I was his girl for a while . . . when I thought he was charmin' and everything. And he's good-lookin' as hell, but it wasn't until I found out how . . . how the Davises are. They're all sort of . . . mean, and they treat women bad. I don't know how the old man treats his wife, but his boys must have learned to mistreat women from somebody."

"The apple don't usually fall far from the tree," Stewart James said.

"It looks like we've got a problem," Clint said. "Sheriff, the four men who have been following us have been at it for weeks."

"Why haven't they tried to take you?"

"Well, my theory is they've been waiting for the right moment, or waiting for help."

"So maybe these five fellas who came to town earlier this week are the help they been waitin' for?"

"It could be."

"Who are the fellas following you?"

"A man named Foreman, and three others. My information on Foreman is that he has a reputation among bounty hunters, but I'd never heard of him until all this started."

"I haven't heard of him, either."

"Do you know the names of the men who are in town?" Clint asked.

"One's Cord, another one's named Sam Libby, and their leader is a fella named Maxim."

"Wade Maxim?"

"You know him?"

"I know of him," Clint said, "and Sam Libby, too. Sheriff, I think we've got a different situation on hand than we thought. A *whole* different situation."

THIRTY

"What do you mean?" Sheriff James asked.

"Well, I don't believe that Maxim and his men are here to meet Foreman and his men," Clint said. "I think what we have here are competing bounty hunters."

"But how did Maxim know that you and Jill would be in Turnback Creek?"

"From what I understand about Maxim's methods, he uses the telegraph and the railroad quite a bit. I think he must have gotten word from someone about our progress, probably by telegraph, and then he must have plotted our course southward and decided that this was where he could intercept us."

"I see."

"Just by coincidence," Clint added, and he hated using that word, "this is where I decided that we should turn and face Foreman and his men."

"How soon will they be here?"

"I'd say within minutes, if they're not already here," Clint said.

127

"I think you and Jill better stay here while I check," James said. "If Foreman and his men intend to stay, they're going to have to register at the hotel."

"I assume there's only one in town?"

"That's right," James said.

"So Foreman and his men will be staying at the same hotel as Maxim and his men."

"That's the way it would have to be," the sheriff said. "Maybe that'll help you. Maybe they'll take care of each other."

"That's a possibility, I guess," Clint said, "but I don't think that Jill and I should stay here at your place, Sheriff."

"Why not?"

"I don't want to endanger your family."

"I'm the sheriff—"

"I know that," Clint said, interrupting him, "and I'm happy to accept your help, but I don't want to risk your family."

"Where do you intend to stay, then?"

"Where everyone else is staying," Clint said. "At the hotel."

"What?"

"We can't—" Jill started.

"We've already determined that they want Jill alive," Clint said. "Her life is not in danger here, unless there's shooting and she's struck by a stray bullet."

"What about your life?"

"I'm not sure," Clint said. "I think Foreman would like to kill me, but he knows he'd need help, and I'm not sure he thinks his men are up to it."

"And Maxim?"

"Maxim is different from Foreman."

"How?"

"He's older, and he's more of a professional, I think. Of course, there's Sam Libby."

"What about Libby?"

"He's got a reputation with a gun," Clint said. "He's a tough man."

"So, you think Libby would like to try you."

"I'm sure he would."

"And would Maxim let him?"

"If it didn't interfere with collecting his bounty. What's this Cord like?"

"Young, antsy," James said. "I had to take his gun away from him one time, to teach him a lesson."

"Sheriff," Clint said, "you'll forgive me for asking this—I hope—but how are your skills with a gun?"

"Adequate—" he started to say, but they were interrupted by Emily James, who reentered the house at that moment.

"Better than adequate, to be sure," she said, attracting the eyes of all three of them.

"Emily . . ." Stewart said.

"Mr. Adams, there was a time when my husband was quite good with a handgun. He stopped wearing one, however, to please me. He now only carries a rifle, when he needs to carry a gun at all, and he's quite an excellent shot with it."

"Is that true?" Clint asked James.

"I can generally hit what I aim at."

"All right, Sheriff," Clint said, "this is what I suggest we do—" He looked at Jill. "And I think we should all be agreed on this."

"Well, let's hear it," James said.

"Yes," Jill said, "let's."

Clint took his time explaining his plan, and both the sheriff and Jill listened quietly until he was done.

"What do you think?" he asked.

Jill was the first to speak.

"I think it sounds like you're the one who's going to be at the most risk."

"That's okay," Clint said. "I can handle the risk. What do you think, Sheriff?"

"I think it's just like any plan of action," James said. "If it works, it's good."

"Well, then," Clint said, "we'll just have to try to make sure it works."

THIRTY-ONE

Clint and Jill left the sheriff's house, mounted their horses, and rode back into town to the hotel. Clint felt sure that Foreman would have kept his men out of town until they could determine what Clint's plans were. He figured once they went to the livery stable and then to the hotel to register, Foreman would bring his men in.

There were a lot of intangibles to consider when formulating his plan. Clint had no idea how Maxim and Foreman—and their men—were going to react to each other's presence. Frankly, he was surprised that Maxim would even involve himself in this. The price on Jill must have been extremely high, which brought up another question. Was she even now telling the whole truth about the Davis family and why Roy Davis wanted her?

Clint's plan was to stay right in the midst of all these bounty hunters, so that if any of them started something they'd all be caught in the cross fire. Maybe they'd even consider the possibility that Jill might be hit by a stray bullet.

"And what do you plan to do once you're in their midst?" Sheriff James had asked him.

"Well," Clint replied honestly, "I'm afraid I don't have that part of the plan figured out quite yet, Sheriff."

Now, as they rode to the hotel, Jill said to him, "I trust you."

"What?"

"I said I trust you, Clint. I know you'll come up with a plan to get us out of here."

"Honey," he said, "I wish the only problem we had was getting out of here. We'd just leave."

"Then why don't we?"

"Because they'll keep coming," Clint said. "From what you've told me about this Roy Davis, he'll keep the price on your head until you're brought back to him."

"I think that's true."

"Then we've got to take care of this situation, and then go and see Roy Davis."

"We have to *what*?"

"If he's not going to take this price off without seeing you, we'll have to go and see him and convince him to remove it."

"I don't see how you can do that, Clint."

"We'll worry about it when the time comes," he said, as they passed the hotel. There were two men out in front, and while Clint didn't recognize either, he recognized the type.

"Are they—" Jill started to ask.

"Don't even look at them," Clint said, interrupting her, "let's just keep riding to the livery and take care of the horses."

Jill did as she was told, but not without difficulty. It was very hard not to look at someone you knew was looking at you.

The two men in front of the hotel were Wade Maxim's other men, Harry Weeks and Dean Emerson.

"Is that her?" Weeks asked.

"She fits the description," Emerson said.

"Wow," Weeks said, "she sure is pretty."

Emerson, who was thirty-one, looked at Weeks, who was in his mid-forties, and said, "She's too young for the likes of you, Weeks."

"Oh, yeah?" Weeks asked. "What about the fella with her?"

Emerson laughed.

"If that's Clint Adams it don't matter how old he is," he said. "He's got a reputation."

"Clint Adams, huh?" Weeks said. "The Gunsmith. You think Sam can take him?"

"I don't know," Emerson said. "I've seen Libby's move, but I don't know."

Wade Maxim came out of the hotel at that point.

"What are you two looking at?" he asked.

"Is that him, Wade?" Emerson asked, jerking his head in the direction of Clint and Jill.

Maxim stepped out to take a look at the two riders who had already passed.

"Can't tell from the back," Maxim said, "but from the looks of that horse it sure seems like it—and the blond hair on the girl."

"She's real pretty," Weeks said.

"Too much of a coincidence for it not to be them," Maxim said. "Let's get over to the saloon and find Sam and Cord. Looks like we might finally have some work to do."

"Vacation's over," Emerson said.

"You can say that again," Wade Maxim said.

THIRTY-TWO

Jill turned in her saddle, no longer able to resist looking back.

"Jill—"

"They're walking away," she said.

"How many?"

"Three now."

Clint turned and looked himself. From behind he could not identify any of the men. He didn't know Maxim that well. He'd have to see the man from the front in order to properly identify him.

"Okay," he said, turning back, "they know we're here. Let's get the horses taken care of and get registered at the hotel, and then we'll see what happens."

Foreman had come into town alone, as he had done in Dexter. As he did, he saw a couple of things of interest. One, Clint Adams and Jill Church were just riding down the street, which seemed odd to him. They had a big enough lead on Foreman and the others to have their horses in the livery by now, if they were planning on staying. He left his horse at the north end of the town—such as it was—and began to follow on foot. He took up short, however, when he saw the men in front of the hotel. Two of them, men he didn't know, but men who showed great interest in Clint and Jill.

He watched and waited, and his patience paid off. He saw Wade Maxim step from the hotel, speak to the two men, and then step out into the street to look after the two riders. After that he and the two men turned and headed the other way. Foreman waited until they went into the saloon, then hurried down the street to check and see if Clint and Jill were leaving their horses in the livery.

It didn't surprise Foreman that Wade Maxim and his men were in town. He'd been expecting to run into them somewhere along the way, given the size of the price on Jill Church.

Foreman knew Wade Maxim's reputation well. In fact, he hoped to someday surpass it. Maxim was legendary when it came to bounty hunters, having almost achieved the status of a Jake Benteen, although not quite. Jake Benteen was top of the line when it came to bounty hunters.

When Foreman reached the end of the street he saw the livery. Clint and Jill were nowhere in sight, so they must have been inside. Either that or they had just kept on going right out of town.

He closed the distance between himself and the livery and stopped by the front door. It took only one quick look inside to tell him what he wanted to know. Clint and Jill were unsaddling their horses. They were staying.

He retraced his steps through town, stopping briefly to look into the saloon. Maxim was there with the two men from the hotel, and two other men. The only one Foreman recognized was Sam Libby.

He now knew all he needed to. It was time to go and get the others.

The fun was about to start.

THIRTY-THREE

"Maxim's here?" Collins asked. "Great, just great."

"Now what do we do?" Willis asked.

"What can we do with Maxim here?" Munch asked.

"We do what we came to do," Foreman said. "We take the girl."

"From Maxim?" Munch asked.

"From Maxim," Foreman said, "and from Adams."

"Yeah," Willis said, "right."

"Wait a minute," Collins said. "Is Libby with him?"

"*Sam* Libby?" Willis asked.

"Libby's there."

"We're gonna take the girl from Adams, Maxim, *and* Sam Libby?" Munch asked.

"I am," Foreman said, looking at them each in turn, "with or without you. I really don't care which. In fact, I'd rather do it without you. That way I get all the money that's on the girl's head."

"Wait a minute," Collins said, "I've come too far to give up on that money. I've got too much time invested in this."

"And you two?" Foreman asked.

"Well . . . yeah, I got a lot of time invested," Willis said.

"Are you in, Willis?" Foreman asked.

Willis frowned, but said, "Yeah, yeah, I'm in."

"Munch?"

"I ain't givin' up my part of the money," Munch said. "You think we can pull this off, Foreman?"

"I know we can."

"Maybe we should, I don't know, wait awhile longer," Munch said.

"We don't have any more time," Foreman said. "To tell you the truth, with Maxim and his bunch here, we may have already waited too long. We've got to do this here and now, in Turnback Creek. We don't have any more choices."

"Okay, then," Guy Collins said, "what do we do first?"

"First we ride into town and register at the hotel," Foreman said.

"A town this size ain't gonna have but one hotel," Collins said. "Maxim and his boys will have rooms there."

"I know that," Foreman said. "Also, Adams and the girl will be there."

"Jesus," Willis said, "we'll all be under one roof."

"Like sticks of dynamite," Munch said.

"Dynamite needs a fuse to set it off," Foreman said.

"Yeah," Collins said, "and who's gonna be that fuse?"

Foreman smiled and said, "I am."

THIRTY-FOUR

The hotel was empty enough for Clint and Jill to get their own rooms, but they registered in one, anyway. Clint assumed that Maxim would have his own room while his men had to share. From the looks of the register, there would also be rooms for Foreman and his men. The Turnback Creek Hotel was having a boom week.

After they checked in, Clint and Jill went right to the room. As they entered she dropped the saddlebags that had come with her new/used saddle and hugged herself, as if she were cold.

"I feel like I'm in the midst of a nest of rattle-snakes."

"Try and relax."

"It's a feeling I've had before, Clint," she said, "and I don't like it."

"You mean in Roy's house?"

She nodded.

"He's the kind of man who keeps other men around him all the time," she said, "and they do whatever he tells them to do."

"Then why didn't he send some of them after you?" he asked.

"That's not a question I can answer."

"Can't answer," he said, "or won't?"

She turned to face him.

"I know I've lied to you more than I've told the truth, but I told you and Sheriff James the truth, and I'm telling you the truth now. I don't know the answer to that question. All right?"

"All right."

She dropped her arms to her sides.

"What do we do now?"

"Well, I suggest you get some rest."

"What are you gonna do?" she asked. "You're not gonna leave me here, are you?"

"No," he said, "the one thing I'm not going to do while we're in this town is leave you alone."

Suddenly she came into his arms and wrapped her arms around him. He held her tightly for a few minutes without speaking.

"You get some sleep and I'll stand watch. With my name in the register I'm curious to see what everyone's reaction is going to be."

"Do you think they'll come up here?"

"They might," he said.

"To get me?"

"Maybe just to talk to me," he said. "Jill, all of these men are professional bounty hunters—some more professional than others." He was speaking of Maxim. "I think that before they try to take you away from me, they'll try to bargain with me."

"Bargain?"

"Maybe offer me a piece of the pie."

"Pie—oh, you mean the money?"

"I mean the money. I'll turn them down, of course, and then we'll have to see what they try next."

He walked her to the bed and sat her on it.

"Here," he said, "let me help you." He crouched down and pulled off her boots.

"Why don't you just come to bed with me?" she asked, reaching for him.

He kissed her warmly, but then moved away from her.

"None of that, young lady," he said. "You'll only distract me. Now, lie down and get some sleep. I'll wake you in a little while and we'll go get something to eat."

"All right."

She curled up on the bed and, not surprising to Clint at all, she was asleep in minutes.

There was a straight-backed wooden chair in the room, and he took it and set it by the window so he could look down at the street. After about twenty minutes he watched as Foreman and his men rode past, on their way to the livery. After that they'd be taking rooms in the hotel.

Now the fun would start.

THIRTY-FIVE

"I don't believe it," Dean Emerson said. He was standing at the doors to the saloon, looking out.

"What?" Maxim asked.

"You'll never believe who just rode by."

"Who?" Maxim asked, annoyed. He was in no mood for guessing games, or surprises.

"Foreman," Emerson said. "Foreman, Guy Collins, and those other two losers he rides with."

Maxim looked over at the bar, where Sam Libby was leaning. This was no surprise to either one of them.

"Want me to talk to him?" Libby asked.

Maxim opened his mouth to say no, then abruptly changed his mind.

"That's a good idea, Sam," he said instead. "I'll talk to Adams, and you talk to Foreman."

"What's there to talk to Foreman about?" Weeks asked.

Libby pushed away from the bar.

"I can try to get him to leave peacefully."

"And if not?" Emerson asked. "If he doesn't agree to that?"

Libby looked at Maxim.

"There's no way we're lettin' Foreman and his bunch have this bounty." Maxim looked at Libby. "Give him a chance to get settled in and then go and talk to him."

"What about Adams?"

"If I go over to talk to him now, I'll run into Foreman checking in," Maxim said. "If that happens I might have to kill him right there and then."

From his vantage point Clint saw a man walk down the street toward the livery. Although he'd only seen the man once before, he recognized him. It was Sam Libby. Libby had a reputation with a gun. Was Maxim sending him to talk to Foreman, or was there another reason?

Maxim had a reputation as a methodical man, a man who did not resort to violence first, as many other bounty hunters did. Clint felt that Maxim was just a step or two below Jake Benteen as far as bounty hunters went.

Clint still didn't know much about Foreman, beyond the little that Rick Hartman's telegram had told him.

He decided that if Maxim didn't come to him before dinner, then he would go to Maxim. If nothing else, he might find out more about Foreman from him. He was sure Maxim would know Foreman well, as a competitor if nothing else.

He looked over at Jill, who was sleeping peacefully, probably for the first time in weeks. He wondered what

Sheriff Stewart James was doing right at that moment. He knew for a fact that the man meant to talk to Foreman, just as a matter of formality.

James was the joker in the deck Clint was playing with. He had no idea how much he could count on the man, and had only this short acquaintance with which to judge the man. If pushed to it—and he probably would be—he decided that he'd trust the man to watch his back. He'd have to, part-time lawman or no. This was the place he'd chosen for his play, and he was going to have to work with what he had, and do the best he could.

For a split second he entertained the thought of going down to the livery to see what was going to happen between Libby and Foreman, but he had promised Jill he wouldn't leave her, and he intended to keep that promise.

He kept his ear cocked for the sound of shots.

Libby walked up to the livery and entered. Foreman and his men were unsaddling their own horses, as Libby, Maxim, and the others had had to do, as well. In the five days Libby had been in town he had never seen a liveryman.

He walked in, and the first one to see him was Ben Munch.

"Holy shit," Munch said, and went for his gun.

"Hold it!" Foreman said, grabbing the man's gun arm.

"That's Sam Libby!"

"I know who it is, Munch," Foreman said. "Relax, okay? Just take it easy."

He released his hold on Munch's arm and approached Libby. As Guy Collins, Willis, and Munch watched, the two men shook hands, surprising the three of them.

"Foreman."

"Good to see you, Sam. Why'd you pick this place?"

"All they have is a part-time lawman," Libby said. "He shouldn't get in the way."

"That's good," Foreman said. "Adams is in town. Have you seen him?"

"No, I haven't, but Wade has."

"How is Wade?" Foreman asked. "Ready to be taken?"

"Maybe," Libby said.

"Just maybe?"

"I'm not sure, Foreman," Libby said.

"I am," Foreman said. "He's past it, Sam. You believe it, too, or you wouldn't be here, would you?"

"No, I guess not."

"Good," Foreman said, "now that we've got that settled, are you ready for Adams?"

"Sure."

"I don't believe it," Collins said.

Both men turned to look at him.

"You turned Sam Libby away from Maxim?"

"Maxim is on his way out, Guy," Foreman said. "I intend to take his place as the best in the business."

"Jake Benteen might have something to say about that," Libby said, and then added, "or me."

Foreman looked at Libby.

"Benteen's over-the-hill, too," Foreman said. "And you? Well, Sam, you're a legend. What can I say?"

"Just tell me that you'll keep your men under control until the time comes."

"Don't worry," Foreman said. "You do your part, I'll do mine, and they'll do theirs. Do we have anyone else?"

"A youngster named Cord," Libby said. "He was on the fence, but Maxim humiliated him earlier today. That was all he needed. He's in."

"Hey," Willis said, "are we sharing the money with two other men?"

"Don't worry about the money, Willis," Foreman said. "Your end won't change."

"It better not."

It wouldn't, Foreman thought, since he didn't intend to give the man an end—him or Munch. They were out, and Sam Libby and his young friend Cord were in.

"I better get back," Libby said. "Wade is gonna talk to Adams later."

"Good," Foreman said. "We'll be around."

The two men shook hands and Sam Libby left. Foreman walked back to his horse.

"When did you turn Libby?" Collins asked.

"Sam and I have known each other a long time." He looked at Munch. "I saved your life, you know. He would have killed you."

"Maybe," Munch said gruffly.

Foreman laughed.

"No maybe about it, Ben," he said. "You would have been a dead man."

Munch mumbled something and continued to care for his horse.

"So Libby is gonna handle Maxim? And Adams?"

"Just Adams," Foreman said. "I'll handle Maxim, myself."

"You fancy yourself up to that, Foreman?" Collins asked.

"Oh, yeah, Guy," Foreman said, "I fancy myself up to it."

He removed his saddle from his horse and put it aside, then turned to the three men.

"You three have to be ready to move when I say so, and not before," he said. "I don't want anybody jumping the gun—hear me, Ben?"

"I hear."

"Willis?"

The man nodded.

"Guy, you're gonna have to watch these two."

"Don't worry," Collins said, "they'll do their part."

"And you do yours, Guy," Foreman said. "If we all do our parts, when this is all over we'll have the girl, and the money. I guarantee it."

"I'd feel a lot better about all this if the Gunsmith wasn't involved."

"Don't worry," Foreman said, "we'll handle him, as well. Don't worry, I've got it all planned."

THIRTY-SIX

No shots.

Clint saw Sam Libby walking back from the livery stable, and there had been no shots. So Maxim had sent his man to talk to Foreman. There was no way Maxim was going to give this bounty up to Foreman. Maybe he and Jill should just stay in their room and see if Maxim and his boys would take care of Foreman and his bunch, and vice versa.

"Clint?"

He turned away from the window and smiled at her.

"What's going on?"

"Nothing," he said. "It's a small town, and nothing's going on. You're supposed to be asleep."

"I'm hungry."

"Well, the hotel has a dining room. I don't know how the food is, but we can try it."

"I don't care," she said, sitting up and swinging her feet to the floor, "right now I'd eat one of my boots if I had to."

"You won't have to," he assured her, "but you *will* have to put them on if we're going to go downstairs."

149

While she did so he looked out the window again and saw Foreman and his men walking toward the hotel.

"What is it?" she asked, moving next to him. "Oh, they're here."

"Yup," Clint said. "You didn't sleep long."

"But I slept well. What should we do?"

"Let's just wait awhile, until they've checked in. We don't want to run into them in the lobby right away."

"They'll be on this floor."

"Right," Clint said. "We should be able to hear them go into their rooms."

He went to the door and opened it a crack. After a few moments they heard movement, footsteps, and then two doors opening and closing.

He turned to her and said, "Let's go and eat."

They might as well have been eating boot leather, as far as Clint was concerned, but Jill seemed to be devouring her steak with no problem.

"I wonder when the sheriff will talk to Foreman and his men."

"As soon as they come out of their rooms, I imagine," Clint said, "whether they come in here to eat, go to the saloon, or find a whorehouse—if this town has one." He stopped talking as he saw a man appear in the doorway.

"What is it?"

"Maxim. Don't turn around."

"Don't worry."

Wade Maxim was standing just in the doorway. He made a show of looking around the room, even though Clint and Jill were the only ones in it.

"Is he coming?"

"Not yet . . . now he's coming."

"What do we do?"

"You keep eating," he said. "I'll do the talking. I'll introduce you, but all you have to do is smile and look pretty."

"I'll see if I can manage that."

Maxim suddenly appeared at their table, and Jill caught her breath. He wasn't particularly large, or good-looking, and he wasn't that scary-looking, but something about Wade Maxim demanded your attention.

"Clint Adams."

"Hello, Wade."

"You remember me."

"That's right, I do."

"Good. That'll make things easier." The man looked at Jill then. "I assume this is Jill Church?"

"That's right."

"Nice to meet you, ma'am."

Jill looked at him and tried a smile. It didn't come out very well.

"Mind if I sit?" Maxim asked.

"Be our guest."

"I hope I'm not spoiling your dinner," Maxim said as he sat.

"I don't think anybody could do that," Clint said, "as well as the food itself is."

Maxim made a face.

"I know what you mean. I've been here five days, and I haven't had a decent meal yet."

"Well, we don't intend to be here that long," Clint said.

"No," Maxim said, "I didn't think you did."

"Tell me something, Maxim."

"Sure, Adams, what?"

"Why have you sunk this low?"

"And how low have I sunk?"

"Hunting a young woman for money."

"A *lot* of money," Maxim said. Then he looked at Jill and added, "Sorry, miss."

"It's not even a legal bounty," Clint said. "She hasn't broken the law."

"Is that what she told you?"

"Yes."

"And you believe her?"

"Yes."

"I didn't break any laws," Jill said harshly.

Maxim looked at her, then at Clint, then pulled a piece of paper from inside his shirt. It was folded four times. When Maxim unfolded it and handed it to Clint, he saw that it was a wanted poster. Clint held it and read it, then looked at Maxim.

"What is it?" Jill demanded.

"Can I?" Clint asked Maxim.

"Hey," the bounty hunter said, "be my guest."

Clint handed the poster to Jill. There was a likeness of her drawn on it, and below her face was the amount of the bounty, and her offense. It was also said that she was wanted alive.

"I never—" she said, but Maxim cut her off by grabbing the poster from her hand. "Clint, you gotta believe me. It's a lie."

"Want to hand her over now, Adams?" Maxim asked, refolding the poster and tucking it back inside his shirt.

"Not just yet, Maxim."

"Still not convinced?"

"No."

Maxim frowned.

"You wouldn't be planning to hand her over to Foreman, would you?"

"No."

"That's good," Maxim said. "That would get me mad, at you and at Foreman. If that happened . . . well, someone might get hurt."

"You do your own killing these days, Maxim, or do you send Sam Libby to do it?"

"Well," Maxim said, unprovoked, "I guess that all depends on his mood and my mood at the time, doesn't it?"

"This girl doesn't deserve to be hunted, Maxim."

"According to this poster," Maxim replied, tapping the paper inside his shirt, "she does."

Abruptly, he stood up.

"I'll give you the rest of today to make up your mind, Adams."

"Meanwhile," Clint said, "I guess you'll have to get it straight with Foreman who gets to try to collect."

"We'll work it out," Maxim said. "Don't worry about that. I'll see you around." He looked at Jill. "Miss, it's nothing personal."

With that he turned and left. Jill had dropped her fork, losing her appetite when she saw that poster.

"Clint, I swear to you that poster is a lie. Roy bought it."

"He'd have to buy a lawman along with it, Jill."

"He's got the money."

"That poster was federal," Clint said. "Does he have *that* much money?"

"Yes."

Clint remained silent.

"Clint, I swear," she said again, "it's a lie."

All he had to do to believe *her* was to believe that Roy Davis—or his father—had the money to buy a phony federal warrant saying that she was wanted for murder.

THIRTY-SEVEN

"Who am I supposed to have killed?" Jill asked.

"The poster didn't say."

"Doesn't it usually?"

"Sometimes."

"There's a telegraph office here, you said," Jill said. "We can find out who I'm supposed to have killed. Can't we do that?"

"We can try," Clint said. "You finished eating?"

She made a face and said, "Probably for the week."

"Then let's go."

When Wade Maxim left the hotel dining room he went up to his room rather than outside. He was convinced by the look on Clint Adams's face that the man had had no idea what the girl was wanted for. Given enough time, he felt sure Clint Adams would make the right decision.

Now all he had to worry about was Foreman, who at that moment was probably in a room in the hotel.

Maxim went to the window and looked out in time to see Clint Adams and Jill Church leaving the building. As he watched he guessed that they were headed for the telegraph office.

They were in for a surprise.

When Clint and Jill reached the telegraph office, they found the door locked tight.

"Is he away for lunch or something?" Jill asked anxiously.

Clint peered inside.

"From the looks of things he's been gone a lot longer than that."

"Damn!" she said. "I wonder if it still works."

"The telegraph key is no good without an operator," Clint said.

"Can't you do it?"

He looked at her.

"Operating a telegraph key is not something you just pick up along the trail, Jill. No, I don't know how to do it."

"Damn!" she said again, stamping her foot.

"Take it easy."

"I'm telling you the truth!" she shouted. "I didn't kill anyone."

"Okay," Clint said, "I believe you."

"You do?"

"Yes."

"Why?"

"Because you're too angry about this not to be telling the truth, Jill."

She closed her eyes for a moment, then opened them and said, "Thank you."

"What's important," Clint said, "is whether or not Maxim believes the poster."

"Why wouldn't he?"

"Well, at the bottom it said you were wanted alive," Clint explained. "If you were wanted for murder, I think it would have said dead or alive, don't you?"

"So you think he knows it's a phony?"

"Maybe."

"Then why's he after me?"

"I'm sure the money is real, Jill," Clint said. "That may be all he cares about."

"What about the other man?"

"Foreman?"

She nodded.

"Do you think he knows it's a fake?"

"I don't know," Clint said. "I'm betting that Maxim's experience will work in our favor here. Foreman is not as experienced."

"So what do we do?"

Clint stared at the locked door of the telegraph office.

"Let's talk to Sheriff James," he said finally. "Maybe there is someone in town who can operate a key."

"Do you think so?"

"No," he said, "but I hope."

THIRTY-EIGHT

Sheriff James, at that moment, was entering the hotel. On the way in he passed Maxim, who was leaving.

"Mr. Maxim."

"Well," Maxim said, "if it isn't temporary Sheriff James."

"Part-time sheriff," James corrected him.

"That's right. Forgive me. How are you?"

"I'm fine, just fine," James said. "Except that—well, maybe you can help me with something."

"If I can."

"There's a stranger in town—another stranger, that is—by the name of Foreman. Do you know who he is?"

"I believe I do, Sheriff. You won't be happy to hear this, but he's a bounty hunter."

"Another one? Is he the friend you were waiting for?"

"I'm afraid not. I'm afraid Mr. Foreman and I are not friends."

"Uh-oh," James said. "That sounds like there could be trouble."

"Well," Maxim said, patting James on the shoul-

158

der, "I'll do everything I can to avoid trouble. That I promise."

"I appreciate that, Mr. Maxim."

"I like to cooperate with the law whenever I can, Sheriff," Maxim said, then added, "even when it's only the part-time law."

"Thanks for your help," James said. He went into the lobby as Maxim stepped into the street.

James approached the front desk.

"Afternoon, Sheriff," the nineteen-year-old clerk said.

"Afternoon, Andy. You got some new guests today."

"Oh, yes," Andy said, smiling, showing a remarkable amount of missing teeth for someone as young as he was, "we're having a good week."

"Let me see the register."

"Sure thing, Sheriff."

James read the names on the page and noted that Foreman was in room four, in the front. He was sharing the room with a man named Guy Collins.

"Did these men talk to you when they arrived?" James asked, pointing to the names.

"They sure did. Asked about food. They should be coming down to the dining room soon."

"The dining room, huh? That's good, real good."

"You gonna talk to them, Sheriff?"

"That's what I'm gonna do, Andy," James said. "I'm gonna talk to them."

"Is there gonna be trouble, Sheriff?" Andy asked hopefully. "Nothin' ever happens in Turnback Creek."

"Andy," James said, "I'm just hopin' to keep it that way."

THIRTY-NINE

Clint saw Sheriff James coming out of the hotel. He grabbed Jill's arm and tugged her across the street.

"Sheriff James!"

James looked up at the sound of his name.

"I'm waitin' for Foreman and his men to come down to the dining room. I'll talk to them there."

"That's fine," Clint said.

"And I just saw Maxim. He said he and Foreman were not friends, but that he would try to avoid any trouble."

"Well," Clint said, "I don't know just how he plans to do that. He's given me the rest of the day to decide what I want to do."

"Does he really expect you to give Jill to him?" James asked.

"I don't think so. Listen, Sheriff, is there anyone in town who knows how to run the telegraph key?"

"There sure is."

"That's great!" Jill said happily.

"Who is it?" Clint asked.

"My daughter."

160

"Rachel?" Jill asked, surprised.

James nodded.

"The former key operator was a youngster about nineteen. I think he had a crush on Rachel and taught her how to run the key. That was last year, before his family up and left town. I think his name was Chuck."

"Sheriff," Clint said, not caring what the former key operator's name was, "would you let Rachel run the key for us?"

"Sure I would."

"That's wond—" Jill started, but James's next words stopped her cold.

"Can you fix it?"

"What?" Clint asked.

"Since you're askin' for a key operator, I was figurin' you knew how to fix it."

"Fix it?" Jill asked.

"It's not working?" Clint asked.

"Uh-uh," James said. "Blamed thing hasn't been workin' since before Chuck—was that his name?—left. He was supposed to report it, but I guess he never did. Line's been dead for months."

"Well," Clint said, "that solves that problem."

"Sorry," James said.

"Not your fault, Sheriff. Whoa, step aside a bit."

He grabbed James's arm and pulled him aside. Clint had seen Foreman and his men coming down the stairs.

"Should we hide?" Jill asked.

"Hide?" Clint said. "We're with the sheriff, Jill, we don't have to hide. Even if Foreman and his men come out that door they won't try anything, not until they know what the situation in town is.''

"The desk clerk said they'd be goin' into the dining room," James said. "I'll take a look."

He peered inside the door, then turned back and said, "Yep, that's where they're goin', all four of them. I better go in and talk to them."

"All four?" Jill asked. "By yourself?"

"It's my job."

"Without a gun?"

"Well," James said, "I left my rifle at home."

"Jill," Clint said, "you go upstairs and wait in the room."

"B-but you said you wouldn't leave—"

"I'm not going to leave the building," Clint said. "I'm going to stay in the lobby and watch the sheriff, just in case he needs help."

"Well, that's right nice of you, Clint," James said, "but like you said, I don't expect them boys to cause no trouble . . . leastways not yet."

"That's okay, Sheriff," Clint said. "Let's just play it safe, huh?"

"Well, okay," James said. "If that's what you want, let's go get it done."

FORTY

Clint stood just outside the hotel dining room but had to be careful not to be seen. Foreman was sitting so that he could see the entrance and the lobby.

While Clint couldn't see what was going on, he could hear just fine, since the four men were the only ones in the dining room. Sheriff James entered and walked up to their table.

"Can I help you, friend?" Foreman asked.

"My name is Stewart James," the lawman said.

"So?"

"I'm the sheriff here."

"I don't see no badge," Willis said.

"I'm the part-time sheriff," James said.

"What can we do for you, Sheriff?" Foreman asked.

"I was just wondering how long you were going to be in town."

"Just long enough to take care of some business, Sheriff."

"What kind of business?"

Foreman smiled.

"My business."

"Well," James said, "there's a man in town I believe you're familiar with."

"And who might that be?" Foreman asked, wondering if the sheriff was going to tell him about Clint Adams.

"Wade Maxim?"

Foreman sat back.

"Yeah, I know Maxim."

"I believe you fellas are in the same business."

"So?"

"I was just wonderin'—"

"Sheriff," Foreman said, interrupting him, "that is, *part*-time sheriff? Can't we talk about this when I'm not eating?"

"Oh, well, sure, I'm sorry to interrupt your lunch," James said. "I was just hoping that we'd be able to, uh, avoid any trouble—"

Foreman interrupted him again.

"I don't think you and I will have any trouble, Sheriff," Foreman said, "if you stay out of my way."

"Pardon me?"

Foreman leaned forward.

"Out of my way, Sheriff," Foreman said. "Is that hard to understand? Don't get in my way!"

"Now see here—hey, let go—"

Willis and Munch stood up and grabbed ahold of him.

"He don't even have a gun," Munch said.

At that point Clint stepped into the room from the lobby.

"Let him go."

All eyes turned toward him, and he saw the eyes of the two men who were holding Sheriff James widen. It was obvious that both men were going to go for their guns.

"No!" Foreman shouted.

"Touch those guns," Clint said, "and I'll kill you both."

They released the sheriff and stepped back. There was still a possibility they'd go for their guns, simply out of panic.

"Sit down, both of you," Foreman said.

They did as they were told, keeping their eyes on Clint. Guy Collins hadn't moved at all.

"Are you all right, Sheriff?"

"I'm fine," James said.

"Since I'm here, Foreman," Clint said, "we'd better have a talk."

"I said all I had to say to you the first time we met," Foreman said.

"All right, then," Clint said, "I'll do the talking. I intend to leave this town with Jill Church, without you and your friends on our trail."

"And how do you intend to do that?"

Foreman asked. "We're free to travel in any direction we want."

"Except mine."

"And you're gonna stop us?" Foreman asked. "All four of us?"

"Oh, yes," Clint said, "all four of you."

"To stop us," Foreman said, "you'd have to kill us all."

Clint decided to play it as hard as he had to. He smiled.

"That's going to be your call, Foreman," he said. "Of course, you've also got Wade Maxim and Sam Libby to worry about."

"So do you," Foreman said.

"Well," Clint said, "when this gets all sorted out we'll see who has to deal with who, won't we?"

"Yes," Foreman said, "we will."

Clint could see the apprehension on the faces of the other three men, but he was impressed by Foreman's confidence.

"Sheriff?" Clint said. "Do you have anything else to say to these men?"

"Yes," James said, "the first one of you who steps out of line again, like you did here, will end up in jail."

He and Clint turned and walked away, and James added quietly to Clint, "That is, they would if I had a jail."

FORTY-ONE

"That was close," James said when they got outside.

"I have to go back in and see to Jill," Clint said. "Will you be okay?"

"I'll be fine, Clint. Thanks for your help."

"I have a suggestion for you, Sheriff."

"What?"

"Don't leave your rifle at home anymore."

"Don't you think that would provoke—"

"Sheriff," Clint said, "I don't think there's going to have to be much provoking—wait a minute."

"What?"

"Provoking."

James frowned, confused.

"What?"

"Provok—never mind, I just got an idea. Would you be able to keep Jill with you at your house for a while?"

"Of course," James said, "she can stay with Emily and the kids—"

"No," Clint said, "I want you to stay there with her, otherwise I feel we'd be endangering your family."

"And what will you be doing?"

"Provoking."

"Provoking wha—oh, I think I see. If you succeed, you know you'll be in the middle."

"I'll try to duck."

"Will you go up and get her?"

"Yes," Clint said, "I'll bring her to your house."

"I'll be waiting."

"You want me to do *what*?" Jill asked.

"I want you to stay with Sheriff James and his wife, at his house."

"Until when?"

"Until it's all over."

"And when will that be?"

"Hopefully very soon."

"Today?"

"Or tomorrow."

"And will you be coming for me?"

"Yes."

"If you're still alive."

"I will be."

"How do you know?"

"I'm not ready to die yet."

"Clint . . . I don't know—"

"Afterward we'll go and see Roy Davis together," he said. "We'll get it all straightened out."

"How—"

"I don't know how," he said, "not yet. Let's just get past this situation, and then we'll deal with the larger one."

"I don't know—"

"I do," he said, grabbing her arm. "Come on, Foreman and his men are still in the dining room. We'll go out the back. The sheriff is waiting at his house for you."

"This is your big plan?" she asked as he hustled her to the door of the room.

"This is it," he said. "This is what I came up with."

"You're going to be the fuse."

"Yes."

In the hall she said, "But you might not be able to avoid the explosion."

"I'll be fine."

They went down the rear stairs to the back door. Clint was glad that the hotel had both. He hadn't checked first.

Outside they hurried down an alley and came out on the street.

"Won't they come to get me there?" she asked.

"I don't think so," he said. "For one thing, they don't know where he lives."

"They could find out."

"For another," he continued, "he is the law, and as much as they can they operate within the law."

"This could be an exception," she said. "There is a lot of money involved."

"Jill," he said, "I'm doing the best I can. Just go along with me on this. The sheriff will protect you."

She tried to protest a few more times until they reached the sheriff's house. Both James and his wife were waiting.

"Come inside, my dear," Emily said.

"I'm sorry to involve you," Jill said as Emily James put her arm around her.

"That's all right," she said. "My husband has explained everything."

Gently, Emily pushed Jill into the house, then turned to Clint.

"You do what you have to do, Mr. Adams," she said, as Sheriff James went inside, "and thank you for keeping my husband out of the line of fire."

"Just keep him here until I come back, Mrs. James," he said.

"Good luck to you."

"Thank you."

Emily went inside and closed the door, and Clint turned to walk back toward town. He decided to start with Maxim. He'd been thinking about seeing Libby when he was walking to the livery and then walking back. There hadn't even been enough time for a confrontation between him and Foreman—but there had been time for a brief meeting.

That gave him an idea.

FORTY-TWO

Clint found Maxim where he thought he'd find him, in the saloon. The rest of his men were there with him, too, including Sam Libby, who was standing near the bar. Maxim was sitting at a back table by himself.

Clint walked in and took in the scene. Libby stood up straight and put a hand on the young man next to him to stay him. Two other men were sitting at a front table together, and they just stared.

The saloon was small, and Clint's voice carried as if he was standing right next to Maxim rather than across the room from him.

"Mind if I join you?"

Maxim, who was sitting with a bottle of whiskey and a glass, raised the glass and asked, "Why not? Get yourself a glass."

"I'd prefer a beer, if I can get one," Clint said, walking to the bar.

"Come and sit," Maxim invited. "The bartender will draw your beer and Cord will bring it over . . . won't you, Cord?"

"Yeah," Cord said sullenly, "sure."

Clint walked across the room and took the chair to Maxim's left, rather than sitting across from the man. From this vantage point they could both see all of the room.

Cord came over with his beer, and Clint noticed that the young man's hand was shaking.

"This is Cord," Maxim said. "Cord, this is Clint Adams."

Cord didn't look at Clint. He placed the beer down in front of him—carefully, though.

"Don't think that Cord's hand is shaking because he's afraid of you, Adams," Maxim said. Immediately, Cord clasped his hands together to stop them from shaking and walked back to the bar.

"See, Cord and I had a misunderstanding and he's been shaking with rage ever since. He's too afraid of me to do anything about it, though, and he's too stupid to be afraid of you."

"He's young."

"That he is."

"I'd like to talk to you alone, Maxim."

"Go ahead and talk."

"What I have to say is for your ears only."

"This have to do with the girl?"

"And more."

"Sam," Maxim called out, "take the boys for a walk."

Clint hoped that they'd encounter Foreman and his bunch on their walk and solve much of the problem for him before he even got his plan started.

"Let's go, boys," Libby said.

"But I don't think we should leave—" Cord started.

"Don't think, Cord," Libby said, "it's not what you get paid to do. Come on."

Libby herded Cord and the other two men out of the saloon.

"Now, what's this all about?"

"I talked to Foreman a little while ago."

"He make you a better deal?"

"Just between you and me, Maxim, how much do you trust your man Libby?"

"Well, first of all, he's not my man. I mean, he's not like the others. Sam's got a mind of his own."

"That's what I'm talking about."

"What *are* you talking about, Adams? You think there's some reason I shouldn't trust Sam?"

"A man in your business, Wade—can I call you Wade?—shouldn't trust too many people."

"And a man with your reputation, Clint—can I call you Clint?—should be a little more careful who he gets involved with. Where is the girl, anyway?"

"In a safe place."

"And what do you intend to do while she's in a safe place?"

"I don't like Foreman much."

"I don't like him much, myself. So what?"

"He's too confident," Clint said. "He's pretty young himself, not as young as Cord, maybe, but young. I think he should be more nervous, like his men."

"And he's not?"

"He's rock steady."

"Why do you suppose that is?"

"It's been my experience, Wade—and I'll bet yours, too—that when a man is too confident it's because he thinks he knows something you don't."

"I'll go along with that, and I think I know what you're driving at. You think Foreman's turned one of my men, and that's what he knows?"

"Maybe."

"And you think he's turned Sam Libby?"

"He's the one I'd pick," Clint said. "He's got the most experience, but he's young enough to still be ambitious."

Maxim played with his glass on the table.

"I'll tell you the truth, Adams, because I think you and me are alike some."

"Okay."

"I don't trust anybody," Maxim said, "not Sam Libby, not anybody. I think when I sent Sam to talk to Foreman earlier it didn't take nearly as long as I thought it would."

"I saw him going to the livery and coming back, Wade," Clint said, "and I thought the same thing."

"And you're right about him being ambitious," Maxim said. "And there's one more thing he is that makes me not trust him."

"Smart?"

Maxim smiled.

"See, I knew we were alike," he said. "Yeah, smart, but maybe not as smart as he thinks he is."

"And how smart does he think he is?"

Maxim leaned forward and said, "I'll tell you. . . ."

FORTY-THREE

"We gonna let this drag on like we been doin'?" Willis asked Foreman.

Foreman looked at Guy Collins. They were in one of their hotel rooms, discussing their next course of action.

"What do you think, Guy?"

"I think if we want that girl," Collins said, "we're gonna have to take her."

"We can't take her from Adams without handling Maxim first," Foreman said.

"Then let's handle Maxim," Collins said. "Let's do it."

Foreman looked at Willis and Munch.

"It's time," Munch said, and Willis nodded.

"Okay, then," Foreman said, "let's do it."

Clint and Maxim looked up as Sam Libby came back into the saloon with Cord and the others, Harry Weeks and Dean Emerson.

"We're gettin' company," Libby said to Maxim. "Foreman and his men are on the way."

Clint looked at Maxim.

"They're gonna push it now," Maxim said. "You better use the back door."

"Maybe I better stay."

Maxim leaned forward.

"Between Foreman's men and us, whichever survive, you're gonna have to deal with later. If you stay here, you're just gonna get caught in a cross fire."

"I can watch your back."

"That's my job," Libby said.

Clint looked at Libby, then back at Maxim.

"Why don't you just stand over by the bar," Maxim said to Clint.

"Wade—"

"Sam, you and the others spread out around the room."

Cord looked at Libby, who did not look back at him.

"All right," Libby said, "let's fan out."

Clint stood up and walked over to the bar. Leo, the bartender, was more red-faced and scared than ever.

"You better use the back door," Clint said to him.

"Yes, sir," Leo said, "thank you, sir," and he was gone.

Clint decided to take up position behind the bar.

Maxim slid his chair back so that it was flat against the wall and kept his eyes on the front doors.

On the way to the saloon Foreman gave the men their instructions.

"There are five of them and four of us," he said, "but remember that Sam Libby is with us, so don't fire in his direction."

"So then there's five of us and four of them," Willis said.

"Didn't know you were so good at arithmetic, Willis," Foreman said. "That's right. We've got a one man advantage. When we go in, leave Maxim to me and Libby. You take care of the other men."

Foreman was deliberately failing to remind them that Libby had converted the young man, Cord. He'd decided they didn't need Cord. Libby would get over the young man's "accidental" death soon enough.

"I want everyone who isn't with us dead," Foreman said, looking directly at Guy Collins. "Anybody have a problem with that?"

Nobody did.

Inside the saloon Maxim was giving his men instructions.

"I don't want any shooting unless we have no other choice," he said.

"Who decides if we have no other choice?" Cord asked.

"Don't be looking to me to shoot first," Maxim said. "If you do that you'll hesitate, and then you'll be dead. You will each know if you have to shoot or not."

Clint examined each man from his vantage point behind the bar. They looked calm enough, except for the younger man, Cord. He was nervous, and Clint wasn't at all sure that he would know whether he had a choice or not.

But Clint couldn't worry about Cord. He was going to keep his eyes on Sam Libby. He was the key man in all of this. Clint felt that, in the end, he'd be able to deal with Maxim much easier than with Foreman. Maxim might listen to reason, but Foreman had probably already decided how he wanted this all to turn out.

And how it turned out all depended on which side Sam Libby was really on.

FORTY-FOUR

Foreman, Collins, Munch, and Willis entered the saloon and stopped just inside the doors. Their eyes took in the positions of the men in the room. Foreman looked over at Clint, who was behind the bar, and then at Maxim, who was still seated with his back to the wall.

"Maxim," Foreman said.

"Foreman."

"We've got to settle this."

"As far as I'm concerned," Maxim said, "the way to settle it is for you and your men to leave town."

Foreman laughed.

"That's not gonna happen."

"What do you suggest, then?" Maxim asked.

"As I see it, there's only one other way to settle it," Foreman said.

"There's got to be another way."

Foreman shook his head.

"There ain't. I've never known you to share a bounty, Maxim. You're not suggesting that, are you?"

"No," Maxim said, "but there's got to be some other way than . . . this."

"Well," Foreman said, "there ain't."

While they were talking Munch and Willis had been edging away from Foreman and Collins until there was some decent space between them.

From behind the bar Clint watched Libby, who was in a far corner of the room. Clint was shocked when the guns came out and Libby didn't move. Gunfire erupted in the room, but neither Clint nor Libby drew their guns. In fact, they watched each other as the bullets flew around them.

When the shooting stopped, Maxim was still standing, his table overturned in front of him. On the other side of the room Foreman was standing, holding his gun down at his side.

Cord, Weeks, Emerson, Collins, Munch, and Willis were all lying on the floor, dead. What Clint didn't see was that it was Foreman who had killed Willis, shooting him in the back after Willis had killed both Cord and Weeks. Munch had killed Emerson, and then Maxim had killed Munch. Foreman had then shot down Collins.

It was quiet in the room, Maxim and Foreman were both holding their guns down by their thighs.

"Didn't make a move, did you, Sam?" Maxim asked.

"Wade—"

"Never mind," Maxim said. "I've had my doubts about you for some time, Sam. Now you've got your chance to pick sides, once and for all."

"I know what side Sam is on," Foreman said. "Are you ready to make some real money, Sam?"

"I'm ready."

"Holster it, Foreman," Maxim said, and holstered his own weapon.

Foreman stole a glance at Clint.

"What about Adams?"

"Don't worry about him," Maxim said. "He'll have to deal with the last man standing."

"He'll have to deal with me, then. Sam? You cut Maxim in half, you hear?"

"I hear."

"Wade?" Clint said. "Can you take Libby?"

"No," Maxim said honestly. "Not a chance."

Clint moved around from behind the bar.

"Then you take Foreman, I'll take Libby."

"Why are you taking a hand in this, Adams?" Foreman asked. "You're not part of this game."

"I'm not only part of the game, Foreman," Clint said, "I'm the pot—me and the girl. I think I'd like to have a say about who wins me."

Foreman frowned.

"Libby? Can you take Adams?"

"Sure."

Foreman looked at Clint.

"He sounds real confident."

"False confidence has killed a lot of men, Foreman," Clint said, "as you'll find out."

Now Foreman firmed his jaw and looked at Maxim.

"All right then," he said, and went for his gun.

Maxim's bullet struck Foreman in the chest just as the other man was clearing leather. The force of the bullet pushed him out through the batwing doors and into the street where he lay, stunned for a moment, before he died.

Sam Libby turned out to be possibly the best gunman Clint had ever faced. He actually cleared leather and was bringing his gun up when Clint's bullet struck him in the heart, exploding it instantly.

Maxim walked over to where Libby was lying and nudged him with his foot. He kicked the man's gun across the room before he turned to look at Clint.

"And Foreman?" Clint asked.

"Oh, he's dead," Maxim said, "but I'll check him."

Clint went behind the bar and drew two beers while Maxim was outside. When the bounty hunter came back, he handed him a cold mug. They both drank deeply.

"I guess I owe you," Maxim said.

"I guess you do."

Maxim grinned, something he didn't do often.

"That's why you took my part, isn't it?" he asked. "You knew if Foreman was the last one standing he wouldn't deal. You *wanted* me in your debt."

"I took your part because I disliked Foreman," Clint said, "but you're right, it doesn't hurt to have you in my debt."

"Okay," Maxim said, "you win."

"What do I win?"

Maxim finished the rest of his beer and slammed his mug down on the bar top.

"I'll go back and tell the man she's dead."

"What?"

"That's what you want, isn't it?" he asked. "You want Davis to stop looking for her?"

"Yeah, but—"

"This is the only way. What did you have in mind?"

"Talking to him."

"Yeah, right," Maxim said, "that's what I wanted to do with Foreman. No, you won't be able to talk to Davis, not to any of them. Not even the father. They're that arrogant."

"Will he believe you?"

"Oh, yeah," Maxim said, "I'll make him believe me."

"He won't pay you."

"Oh, I'll get him to pay me something," Maxim said. "We'll call it a kill fee."

Maxim surprised Clint by sticking out his hand. Clint shook it.

"What will you do now?" Clint asked.

"I don't know," Maxim said. He looked around. "I'm gettin' too old for this."

He turned and started walking to the doors. When he reached them he turned around and looked at the carnage.

"Can you clear this with the local part-time law?"

"No problem."

Maxim nodded and left.

Clint finished his beer, then left to go and tell Jill that she was free.

Watch for

OUTBREAK

191st novel in the exciting GUNSMITH series
from Jove

Coming in November!